STAY ALIVE

BREAKDOWN

STAY ALIVE

BREAKDOWN

JOSEPH MONNINGER

SCHOLASTIC INC.

ISBN 978-0-545-56355-0

12 11 10 9 8 7 6 5 4 3 2   14 15 16 17 18 19/0

Printed in the U.S.A.

First printing, August 2014

PART ONE

THE MILK TRUCK

SURVIVAL TIP #1

Survival begins in preparation. The better prepared you are, the better your chance at survival. Although it is impossible to anticipate every contingency, general preparedness will always bring dividends. Most disasters can be broken down as follows: approach, endurance, survival. If you carry sufficient food and water for three days, you will stand a good chance of making it through the initial stages of a disaster. Encourage your parents to keep an emergency kit in their automobiles, at home, and on their person when practical. A package of nuts can be both a lifesaving means of nourishment and excellent bait to trap larger animals. A compass is easily transportable and indispensable when needed. Think ahead. Don't assume an extraordinary situation cannot happen to you.

CHAPTER 1

The blackout dropped across the Minnesota north country like a tablecloth being fluffed out and draped over a table. If you had been in a plane and happened to look down, you might have marveled at how smoothly the blackout moved. The largest cities went first, the tall buildings snuffing out like candles in one large huff. The power continued to fade under the spreading darkness, slithering down the center of smaller channels, extinguishing things as it proceeded.

A softball stadium in the town of Blue Earth went dark in the middle of a fly ball.

In Austin, Minnesota, the lights at the local skate park went out a second after a skateboarder jumped on his new deck and headed down the biggest incline in the Sioux Rec Center cement canyon. He had to ride blind.

A thirteen-year-old babysitter on Sidle Street in Little Falls had two arms in the tub washing down a three-year-old when the lights went off in the house. For a second, she did nothing at all. The house went quiet, too quiet, and suddenly the only sound audible was the enormous grandfather clock ticking in the study. It sounded like a heartbeat, it always had, but then it grew louder and louder. She didn't dare move, didn't do a thing except wait for the lights to come back on.

But the lights didn't come back on.

It was the biggest blackout to ever hit Minnesota. It took a snapshot of almost everyone in the state, a giant flash exploding for a second, then freezing everyone in place. The difference was that no one smiled for this picture. They simply gazed up with worried looks, red eyes sizzling for a second before the state plunged into a darkness it hadn't known in more than a century.

At Camp Summertime in northern Minnesota, the blackout didn't have much of an impact. No one bothered to check if the blackout extended beyond the camp. Blackouts happened frequently at Camp Summertime, a result of trees flicking down to snap a line or squirrels eating their way into a transformer. When the power died, as it had on four occasions over the course of the summer, an enormous generator kicked on in the tool shop beside the boathouse and provided backup energy. Blackouts were a fact of life at Camp Summertime. No one imagined it could last more than a couple of hours.

Besides, it was closing day for the camp, the morning after the final bonfire, August 27. Parents had already picked up hundreds of kids, each family unit celebrating a mini-reunion followed by the long slog with sleeping bags and trunks back to the parents' SUVs. Once they departed, the families didn't bother calling back to inform the camp of the generalized blackout. For one thing, they didn't have a sense of how broad and far-reaching the blackout extended. Not at first. No one did. It wasn't until near sunset the next day that the electric company, Minnesota Power and Light, issued a bulletin about the blackout. The bulletin outlined the blackout's unprecedented dimensions, attributing the malfunction to the demand for air-conditioning in the record late-summer heat, but the alerts went out over radio waves, and only people in cars, or ones with battery-powered transistors, received those messages initially. Parents driving away with their kids heard the news, but once they left it didn't occur to them to call back to Camp Summertime. The place passed quickly out of their thoughts as they pointed toward home. Summer was officially over. They had Labor Day picnics and school to think about.

In the confusion caused by the blackout, no one gave a thought to the white commuter van – called the Milk Truck by the campers for the putrid odor of spoiled milk that clung to the interior – that carried the kids who were making plane or train connections a half-day drive's away in International Falls. The kids left in the Milk Truck at ten fifteen in the morning. It was the last van of the season, the last group to leave. Every year, in a joyful ceremony, the owners of the camp, Dave and Margaret Wilmont, toasted the final departure with a bottle of champagne once the Milk Truck disappeared. They raised their glasses to each other, smiled at the knowledge that another successful summer had been completed, then handed the keys to Devon O'Neal, the winter caretaker.

Devon O'Neal was a wannabe novelist who liked the quiet of a winter beside the lake. He spent the dark months in the nurse's apartment, huddled next to the woodstove. Occasionally, he would go ice fishing to break up the monotony, or try to complete a five-part fantasy novel called *Roman Winter* that he had been writing for three years. Devon accepted the keys with a few last-minute instructions, then watched as the Wilmonts climbed into their Otter aircraft and roared up the lake to leave.

When Devon saw the plane disappear at last, he smiled, happy to regain his island of personal isolation. He had a million things to do to shut down the camp and tuck it away for winter, but for the moment he simply wandered around, assessing the damage and the work to be done. Besides, it was devilishly hot, well above ninety degrees, and that simply did not happen in northern Minnesota. He thought about going for a swim or taking a nap. He did not give a thought to the Milk

Truck, the most decrepit van in the fleet and the one with the longest journey across the most isolated road, the only van traveling north toward International Falls. Devon swung the security gate closed on One Hundred Mile Road – the road that took the Milk Truck northward through a couple million acres of Minnesota spruce forest – then he padlocked the gate and turned back to the camp, wondering what he would cook for dinner on this, his first night alone.

CHAPTER 2

The first thought Albert "Flash" Ellsworth, age sixty-three, had when he felt the Milk Truck dying underneath him was, *I told you so*. He had told everyone he could think to tell that the Milk Truck, the van purchased from the St. Paul's school district at least a quarter of a century before, was too darn rickety to trust. Vans were well made, he knew, especially Fords, but all machines made by human hand had an earthly limit. That's what he thought. He had told the bosses of Camp Summertime that the van needed to be junked and a new one bought. But did they listen? Of course they didn't. They told him the Milk Truck was a tradition and a part of camp lore.

No one listened to Flash Ellsworth. That was fact.

But as usual, he was right about what he knew. He didn't pretend to know everything, but he knew engines, and he knew the Milk Truck better than any engine around, and he knew it was dying when they had turned onto One Hundred Mile Road.

He heard one of the kids make a mocking sound – probably Tock, the troublemaker – when the van began to shake, and he glanced in the mirror quickly to tell him to knock it off. The Milk Truck had dignity, he wanted to say, and everything would get old one day, even them, but what good did it do to try and reason with spoiled kids? He shook his head and tried to lift the gearshift into a soft second, but the van kicked and complained and began to grind.

His second thought was, *We're a lot of miles from somewhere, and a few miles from nowhere.*

One Hundred Mile Road wasn't called One Hundred Mile Road for nothing, he knew. That was another thing he would have told Margaret and Dave Wilmont if they had been standing in front of him. He would have said, *You've got a girl here, Olivia, who has to get to International Falls.* Or *You have another one, Maggie, who is going from here to LAX, then onto Japan for some sort of special exchange. Two of the boys, Preston and Simon, are heading out to the East Coast. Bess, too, she was going somewhere.* You do not send a bus filled with kids hurrying to make a connection over One Hundred Mile Road on one of the hottest days of the summer and expect to wave good-bye and hop in your fancy Otter aircraft and head toward the Outer Banks as Dave and Margaret Wilmont did every autumn. You do not lock up the camp, lower the security gate behind the Milk Truck, and wave them off. No, you give them first-class transportation, and you supervise their travel, and you make sure the itinerary makes human sense. But not the Wilmonts. That wasn't the way things went at Camp Summertime.

"Hey!" someone yelled from the back of the van. "Hey, what's going on?"

"Mind your knitting!" Flash said.

"What does that even mean?" Maggie asked.

"It means it's too hot to listen to you kids. Mind your own potatoes."

He didn't know for sure if he was talking to them or to himself or to the Milk Truck.

He gently moved the gearshift back into first and tried to even her out with gas. But the Milk Truck started to shudder even harder. Then it wheezed and bucked, and he knew the party was over. He eased the truck to the side of the dirt road. Not that it mattered if he put her on the side of the road, he reflected. They were the last vehicle coming this way until the snowmobiles took it over in winter. Gates blocked the road from either end – that was a steadfast rule the Wilmonts had instituted many years before – so that no drifters or joyriders could make it out to Camp Summertime and steal whatever they could carry. It was his job to take the last group out, and Devon would lock the door behind them.

He gave the van one more squirt of gas, then listened to it pop three times in quick succession. He turned it off quickly, and silence suddenly filled in the empty places. Then the van jerked a little to the right, and the front tire crumpled on the shoulder of the road. A few trees dragged their bony fingers over the roof of the van, and the forward momentum of the vehicle grinded the van into a dull, teetering halt. They weren't going fast enough to cause any real damage, but the van sank a little on its axle, as if it had settled down to die.

Then the kids began to clap.

"Do you people have any brains in your head?" Flash asked, his anger at the phony applause rising up in him as quickly as a bead of mercury in a thermometer. "Does even one person here have a particle of brain?"

It was too hot for this nonsense. Way too hot. He turned in the driver's seat, his eyes moving over the passengers. He was tired of kids, he realized. It happened by the end of every summer. He felt them growing on him like a mold or fungus. By this time of year, late August, he had a stomach full of them and had little patience left.

"Now be quiet and let me think for a second, would you?"

"Is it broken down?" Quincy asked.

"Duhhhhhhh," Tock said, his voice twisted up to mock Quincy.

Tock was the bad egg, Flash knew, but Quincy had asked a pretty silly question just the same.

"Looks like it," Flash said, getting himself under control. "You can get off the bus and stretch your legs if you want. There's nothing around here, so don't wander off. Is that clear?"

"Camp Summertime strikes again!" Maggie said.

"Is that clear?" Flash asked again, ignoring her and raising his voice so there could be no mistake. The heat wouldn't give him a second to clear his head.

Flash gave them a last look, then swung out of the van and walked to the front of it. He didn't possess the slightest hope that he could repair the engine. Old was old, done was done. But he needed to give a look anyway, and he needed time to think without the kids' eyes on him. He buckled up the hood and climbed onto the front bumper to see into the engine cavity. At the same time, he listened to the kids clattering off the bus. The kids laughed and joked, and Flash made himself bend over the engine so he wouldn't feel compelled to slap them down.

He took one long look at the engine wafting smoke into the air, waiting for a miracle cure to occur to him. He didn't touch anything. There was no point in pretending. The engine was cooked. Done. The Milk Truck had taken its last trip. He smelled a deep, acrid electric burn that he associated with overheating motors. The smell floated like a cloud around the van. Not even a breeze came to push it away.

He stepped down off the bumper. A dull, sick headache started forming along his hairline. He reached in his jacket for his cell phone, but he knew without checking it that they were well beyond cell range. He walked a few feet away and checked it anyway. No bars. No contact, he saw when he looked. He slid the phone back into the chest pocket of his jacket. He looked around, calculating his next step.

This, he realized, was one giant pickle.

Tock threw a rock at a gray squirrel and missed it by a few inches.

The squirrel didn't move. It stayed exactly where it had been a moment before, its pointed face staring at him. Tock didn't expect to hit the squirrel precisely, but it was fun to try anyway. He knew the other kids watched him.

He threw a second rock at the squirrel, and the rock veered away in a left-hand curve. He listened to it rattle off into the brush. The squirrel chattered a little bit then, and Tock hustled to grab another rock. Before he could throw it, Maggie stepped in front of him and refused to move.

"That squirrel hasn't done a thing to you, Tock," Maggie said, her voice tangled and angry. "Leave it alone."

"Get out of the way," he said.

"I don't think so."

"There's no way I'm going to hit the stupid thing," Tock said, feinting a little to one side to get past Maggie. "I'm just playing."

"Play somewhere else," Maggie said, slapping at his arm when he began to throw. He kept his hand out in a stiff-arm to keep her away. He threw a rock, but it was way off. He couldn't even see the squirrel anymore.

"Why are you so mean?" Maggie demanded. "You're mental, you know that? You're really mental. Why would anyone try to hurt a squirrel?"

"It's gone now, anyway. Big deal."

He turned and chucked a rock down the dirt road. It made a couple of skips, then died. He rubbed his hands on his camouflage pants. Squirrels went up a tree in a swirl like the red stripe went up a barbershop pole. He knew that. He walked ten yards down the road, hoping to see the squirrel resting on the other side of the tree. But it had disappeared.

To kill time, he went down onto his hands and toes and did twenty push-ups. It was hot as blazes to be doing push-ups, but he didn't care.

He did them fast and well. He tried to do at least two hundred a day. Most days he did more. He liked the way they made his arms look, the back of his triceps like fat, angry roots, but he also liked the strength gain. He could feel the power when he flexed. He was twelve years old. In six years, a little less, he could join the Marines. That was his dream.

When he finished with the push-ups, he sprang back to his feet. No slow climbing up like an old man for him. He did things crisply, like a Marine.

"Is it cooked?" he asked when he saw Flash going back into the van for something.

Flash didn't answer. He just shrugged.

"We are so stranded!" Tock yelled, and laughed. "We are so burned!"

He looked over at Simon – he always looked over at Simon – put his hands up like claws, and made a scary rumbling sound in his throat.

"Bigfoot's going to get you," he said to Simon.

Simon shook his head harshly from side to side. Then he began to cry.

Bess stepped between Simon and Tock and turned her back to block Tock. *Like a basketball screen*, she thought. Tock never left her brother alone. Not for long anyway. He was like a fly on garbage, or a shark circling, always waiting to torture her brother at the first opportunity. She couldn't count how many times she had stepped between Tock and Simon over the summer. It went on and on and on. The kid was a bully, a semi-dangerous one, she imagined, and he preyed on her brother's weakness.

"It's okay," she said to Simon for the millionth time.

Tock kept making scary sounds behind her. It's what he did. She looked around at some other kids – Maggie and Preston – and understood she would get no help from them. Tock scared them. Tock scared everyone except her and Olivia. The kids stood around in loose clusters, watching. It struck her as ironic that Maggie would intervene to stop Tock from hurting a squirrel but wouldn't bother helping her to stop Tock from hurting her brother.

She put her arm over Simon's shoulders and walked him away from Tock. She walked him toward the edge of the forest. It was strange to her that they could stand on a brown tongue of dirt that went on for miles, but all around her, everywhere, pines stood ready to gobble up the light. It was a little unnerving.

"It's okay," she whispered to Simon. "He just does things like that because he knows he can get a rise out of you. Do you understand? If you don't react, it will take all the fun out of it for him."

Simon nodded.

He suffered from Asperger's syndrome. Well, no, not Asperger's syndrome, Bess corrected herself. The medical profession had changed the name of his diagnosis. It was now called autism spectrum disorder.

Whatever it was called, it was often hard to know what he understood. He had difficulty filtering things.

"We're going to be okay," she said calmly. "There's nothing in the woods that will hurt you, I promise. We're probably going to be broken down here for a little while, but someone will figure out that we haven't made our travel connections and then they'll come for us. No problem. You believe me, right?"

Simon nodded. He could talk, but he usually didn't.

She wanted to say more to reassure him, but then Flash called them back to the van. He stood next to the sliding passenger door and waved them closer. Bess put her arm through Simon's and walked him over. She made sure to station herself on the opposite side of the small gathering from Tock.

Olivia cracked a piece of hard candy between the molars at the back of her jaw. She liked the way the candy exploded even more than the taste really. Actually, she liked everything about Mann's Hard Candy: the little cellophane wrapper that uncurled so easily if you knew how to twist the end just right; the brightness of the candy; the sweet, nearly tongue-numbing flavor of the orange and lime and Hawaiian-punch mango candies; the sugary coating they left on her tongue and lips. She ate a lot of hard candy and kept a few pieces in various pockets on her most of the time. She thought of them as little treats. The dentist warned her about eating so much hard candy, and so did her family physician, but she didn't listen.

She stopped chewing long enough to hear what Flash had to say.

"I guess it's pretty plain to everyone that we're broke down," Flash said, his voice surprisingly reedy for such a beefy man. "And I can't tell you that anyone is going to be on the way to get us anytime soon. They expect us to make it up to International Falls sometime this afternoon. We've come about thirty miles. We probably have close to thirty in front of us."

"I thought it was called One Hundred Mile Road," Maggie asked.

Maggie always asks, Olivia thought. She needed to know everything. She reminded Olivia of a dragonfly that had to land on everything to know it.

"It's called One Hundred Mile Road because it *feels* like a hundred miles to go over it, what with the ruts and everything. It's about sixty miles, give or take. And it goes through a bunch of woods. Nothing between here and there."

"So what do we do?" Maggie asked.

"You do nothing," Flash said. "I'm going to walk back to Camp Summertime and see what I can scare up. I'll make some calls."

"You're going to walk thirty miles?" Tock mocked him. "You go, Flash."

"You have a better idea, Tock?" Flash asked.

"Why not go in the other direction?" Preston asked.

Olivia crunched another piece of candy in her teeth. It was interesting to watch the dynamics. Preston was a goody-goody, kind of the angel, opposite of the devious Tock. She had seen a cartoon once in which a little red devil perched on one shoulder of Bugs Bunny and a little white angel on the other. Tock and Preston could have played the roles without combing the hairs on their heads a bit different. It was fascinating to watch.

"Because I can maybe get the old gray van by going that way and I can call ahead," Flash said. "It's probably closer to go forward, but I can't guarantee I'd find trans-port for you."

"We're not going to make our connections," Maggie said, as if fully understanding the situation for the first time. "That's right, isn't it? I mean, there's no way, right?"

"Not unless someone comes along, and that's not very likely. The road's gated at both ends. Devon and I are the only ones with keys beside the Wilmonts and the police."

"So what are we supposed to do?" Bess asked. "While you're walking, I mean."

"Nothing you can do," Flash said. "Except wait and hang tight. Stay with the van. Someone will come get you eventually. If not me, someone else."

Olivia thought, *Famous last words.* She crunched one of the pebbles of hard candy left in her right cheek. It gave a satisfying crack inside her head.

"We should sue," Tock said, his eyes moving around in search of support. "I mean it."

"Well, you go and sue, big boy," Flash said. "I'll be back as fast as I can. It might take a day or more."

"A day or more?" Maggie yelped. "Are you serious?"

"Serious as a heart attack," Flash said. "You all stay with the van, you understand? Don't leave it. You've got shelter here, and that's the main thing. Just hold tight."

"We don't have anything to eat," Preston said. "And I don't think we have much water."

"I'll tell you what," Flash said. "You can walk, and I'll stay here. How would that suit you?"

Preston didn't say anything. Olivia smiled, not entirely displeased to see Flash stick a barb in Preston's perfect composure.

Flash didn't wait around. He raised his hand in a salute as he left.

"Adios," he said.

No one, Olivia noticed, answered him back.

CHAPTER 3

Quincy stood outside the van, his hand up to shade his eyes from the late-afternoon sun. It was boiling. It was the time of day they used to swim at camp, but now they stood on a road in the middle of the woods during the hottest part of the afternoon.

It was *really* boiling.

He kept his hand up and watched Preston walk around on top of the van. This was the big plan, Quincy knew. The idea was to gain height by climbing on the roof of the van and maybe catch a cell phone signal. It had been Preston's idea, one hatched after everyone had sat in the shade for most of the early afternoon. Quincy had wanted to point out that if it made sense to climb on the van, why not climb a tree instead? A tree was taller, after all, and by their logic they would stand a better chance of getting a signal. But Quincy knew his voice didn't count for much in these kinds of situations. It just didn't. Besides, he preferred not to draw Tock's attention.

So he stood with everyone else and watched Preston hold his phone up in various directions, the van roof making wobbly metal sounds underneath him. It must have been a zillion degrees on the roof, Quincy figured. Preston reminded Quincy of a priest or a rabbi, his hands up as if celebrating a religious service. It was funny to think about it like that if you didn't care that it also meant they were stranded on a road in the middle of a Minnesota pine forest.

"Anything?" Maggie asked.

Preston didn't take his eyes off the phone, but he shook his head.

"Well, don't point it back toward camp," Tock said. "There's nothing back that way."

"There's nothing any which way," Bess said. "There's no signal. No one has had a signal all summer."

"Ginny McCall got one," Olivia said. "She was out on the lake when she got it."

Quincy didn't know if that was true or not. It was part of camp lore that Ginny McCall got one, but who knew for sure? Camp life consisted of a million rumors.

"Nothing," Preston said, bringing the phone to his side. "Not even a bar."

Quincy watched him climb off the van. Preston slid on his butt down the windshield, then took a quick hop and jumped off the engine hood. He landed with a little woof of his air going out. He was showing off, Quincy knew, but that was Preston's way.

"So now what?" Maggie asked.

"Now nothing," Tock said, rubbing his hands together like an arch criminal and making his voice a little crazy. "Unless we decide to eat Simon. How about a little Simon burger? Or a big roll of Simon bologna? With plenty of mayooooooo . . ."

"Leave him alone," Bess said.

Quincy watched Bess walk Simon away from the group. Quincy would have stood up to Tock if he thought he stood a chance. Tock was no joke.

"Does anybody have any food?" Maggie asked. "We should put everything together and see what we have."

"We should put everything together and see what we have," Tock said, mocking her by trying to match her voice. "Come on, everyone. Let's all do what Maggie says."

"We need water," Preston said. "Water is more important than food. As hot as it is, we're going to really need plenty of water."

"We're in Minnesota," Tock said, picking up a stone and chucking it into the woods. "The land of ten thousand lakes, duh."

"Potable water," Maggie said. "Drinkable water."

"Potable? You actually said *potable*? You guys are ridiculous," Tock said. "You make me sick. You're such wimps."

"And what are you? A pretend Marine?" Olivia chimed in.

Tock slowly, slowly turned to look at her. She cracked a piece of hard candy between her teeth. It was strange to see someone call Tock on his junk for once. Honestly, Quincy reflected, Olivia was bigger than Tock and probably stronger. People didn't mess with Olivia. She had a slow, silent strength that got her selected for teams faster than just about anyone in camp. She didn't look athletic, but that didn't mean she wasn't. She had won the Color Games tug-of-war championship, which meant, more or less, that she was the strongest camper in camp. She had bear strength, people said.

"You'll see what I am if you don't shut up," Tock said.

"Anytime," Olivia said, squaring her shoulders. "Bring it."

She didn't change her tone or expression. She simply stared at him. Tock moved his eyes away after a little while. *That was that*, Quincy thought. Hierarchy established. He knew, though, that Tock would try his best to get even. Tock didn't let things slide.

"Is anyone else getting hotter?" Maggie suddenly asked. "I am so sweaty. It's disgusting, this heat."

"I can't believe we're spending the night here," Bess said, slowly walking Simon back to the group. "I mean, that's really happening, isn't it?"

"Flash can't walk thirty miles and get back here tonight," Tock said. "No way. He's going to be sleeping out if you ask me. We're stuck here."

No one said anything. But then Quincy had a brainstorm.

"Why don't we build a fire?" he said. "That would be a place to start. It will give us something to do, and it will keep any animals away."

No one said anything against it, Quincy noted, and that was as much of an endorsement as he was likely to get.

"Collect whatever you have inside," Bess said after a moment. "Any food or water and bring it out. We can see what we have, anyway."

"I'll collect kindling," Quincy said. "Does anyone have a match?"

"I'll check," Olivia said. "I've seen Flash stash some for his cigarette breaks."

"Bring out anything that might be useful," Bess yelled as people headed toward the van. "Even if you're not sure, just bring it, anyway."

Quincy went to the edge of the woods and collected pinecones and twigs. He loved making fires. It was his favorite thing to do at camp.

It isn't much, Maggie thought, kneeling at the edge of the canvas tarp spread on the ground as a collection station. Whatever they had to eat stretched out in front of her.

It isn't much, she thought again.

The trouble was, everyone had cleaned out their stashes to get ready for the trip home. All summer, she knew, they had hundreds of boxes of candy, gum, marshmallows, juice boxes . . . all the good stuff. The food and candy had come in boxes from home, and you could never walk into your cabin without someone holding out a brown box and saying, "Go ahead, my mom sent it."

Brownies, fudge, fresh apples, dried apricots, yogurt-covered raisins. You name it, you could find it.

But now, she repeated to herself, *it isn't much.*

"Is that everything?" Bess asked from her position across the canvas. "I figured we'd have more than that."

"Everyone cleaned out for the trip home," Maggie said. "It's not much."

"We're not going to be here that long," Preston said. "It's not like we're going to die out here."

"It's good to know what we can count on," Olivia said. "Good to know what we have. You need to tally things."

Maggie did a quick inventory.

A half bag of Swedish Fish. A Snickers bar. A six-pack of Cracker Jack. Two cans of diet cola. Ten bottles of spring water. A sleeve of chocolate chip cookies. A pair of bananas so old and black they looked like witches' fingers. A can of cat food. A jar of salmon eggs. A melted and flattened Hershey bar. Half a stick of beef jerky. A can of ravioli. A single-serving-sized bag of dried beans and rice.

One book of matches from underneath the driver's seat.

It isn't much, Maggie thought one final time.

"We could eat a little tonight, divide it up, then save some for tomorrow," Preston said. "We'll be out of here tomorrow."

"Let's eat it all," Tock said, being wild and silly, Maggie knew. She doubted he could help himself. He just said things to say things.

"We should hold it back for a couple days," Bess said. "We shouldn't plan to be rescued right away. You never know."

Maggie saw Olivia nod. Simon nodded, too, but he usually nodded at anything Bess said. Preston didn't comment one way or the other, and Quincy didn't care as long as he had a chance to make a fire. People behaved in predictable ways, she reflected.

"Why don't we make a food committee?" Maggie asked. "The committee could decide how the food should be divvied up."

"A food committee?" Tock said. "For what? We're not on the top of Mount Everest, you know."

"We could start with a handful each of Cracker Jack," Olivia said. "I know I'm hungry. Just a bite."

"We should all drink water, too," Bess said. "Stay hydrated."

"Is this a Scout meeting or something?" Tock asked. He reached over and grabbed a box of Cracker Jack and split the top off it. Then he went around and poured out a handful for each person. It took him three boxes, but at the end he emptied the remaining portion into his mouth. Maggie judged it to be the lion's share, but she didn't say anything because the bite of Cracker Jack was beyond delicious. She didn't want to risk losing the taste of it by talking. She chewed carefully and swallowed only when she had sucked the last bit of flavor out of it.

"Now the fire?" Quincy asked. "It was too hot before, but it's cooling down a little."

"Now the fire," Bess said.

Simon watched the fire.

He had been near fires plenty of times over the summer, but they never ceased to amaze him. He liked the way they moved and danced. He liked how they smelled. Sometimes he could watch a branch or twig take the heat and guess when it would explode into flame. That was an excellent use of his time.

Simon was very concerned about time usually. But a fire lived outside of time, so he didn't count it in the same way.

He sat on the ground. He wore plenty of clothes, too, although it was honestly too hot for the clothes he wore. That had been an excellent use of his time. He felt warm beside the fire. The fire existed down on the ground, and the stars existed in the sky, and he thought the flames could drop down out of the sky as easily as rise up from the earth. That's what he thought, though he knew he couldn't explain that to anyone except Bess. And even she wouldn't understand. Bess knew a lot, but she didn't know everything.

He liked everything about the fire except Tock. Tock lived on the other side of the fire, and his face sometimes turned into the face of a wolf. Tock was a horrible use of time.

"What if Flash doesn't come back?" Maggie asked. "What do we do then? Do we just sit here and wait forever?"

"Do we just sit here and wait forever?" Tock mocked her, twisting his voice the way she did.

Simon believed Tock had twenty or more voices inside him. They ran down inside him, side by side, like two dozen electrical wires that filled up a cable. He could do a Maggie voice better than Maggie could.

"Well, do we?" Maggie insisted on an answer.

"We're better off here beside the van than some-where else along the road," Preston said. Preston sat at three o'clock around the fire. Preston used his time very well, Simon thought. Preston kept his eyes on the fire while he talked.

"We might have to walk out," Olivia said. "We can't depend on Flash making it back to camp."

"He'll make it. Thirty miles isn't that far," Bess said.

"Thirty miles is pretty far," Preston said. "Flash isn't in the greatest shape, you know?"

"He smokes," Bess said.

Simon nodded. That's what he would have said. Flash did not use his time well at all.

"If he makes it back to camp, he can call for help," Maggie said.

"Someone is going to come for us, anyway," Preston said. "People will notice that we didn't show up for our connections. We just have to hang tight. It's really no big deal."

"Unless we starve," Maggie said. "Or unless we get dehydrated and pass out."

"It takes a few days for that to happen," Olivia said, her mouth breaking candy in between words. "The heat should break soon for the night."

"And there should be some water nearby," Preston said. "We can find a clean source."

"We could walk out, you know?" Olivia said. "It could be kind of cool. It would be an adventure."

"It's about thirty miles," Preston said.

"So?" Olivia asked. "We could do it. It might take two days, maybe three. But we could do it. We could just stay on the road. If someone comes along, fine. If not, at least we're getting somewhere. As long as we took some breaks when it was at its hottest, we'd be fine."

"Flash said to stay," Maggie said. "He was clear about that."

Tock threw a big hunk of pine into the fire. He did it just to make sparks, Simon knew. Tock liked anything that broke apart.

"I'm walking out tomorrow," he said. "I don't care what Flash said."

"What will that prove?" Maggie said.

"It will prove that I don't have to spend more time with you," Tock said.

Then he turned to Maggie and made a sick face. When he turned his face back to the fire, Simon made sure not to catch his eye.

CHAPTER 4

Preston had a hard time believing how dark it was inside the van. He had no idea how late it might be, but it didn't feel close to morning. It felt like the fat middle of the night. Now and then he heard people turn and breathe heavily, and once someone muttered something that he couldn't make out. The wind hit the van a few times, but for the most part the sky blinked clear and bright and hot. Part of him wished they hadn't put out the fire. He wanted to sit beside it some more, to watch the woods grow darker and darker, but he understood they needed to bury a fire at the end of a night. That was good woodcraft. His uncle Adam talked a lot about good woodcraft.

He tried to sleep, but sleep wouldn't come. His mind

felt too active, and it was too hot inside the van. It was kind of fun, actually, being stranded like this. At least it was out of the ordinary. Back home, things were not great. His mom and dad were headed for divorce, so he didn't mind the delay in getting back to his everyday world. Even sleeping in a van in the middle of the woods was better than the situation at home, where every word was freighted and packed with double meanings, and the tension crackled around the house like static electricity.

After a while, he gave up trying to sleep. He carefully climbed into the center aisle of the van and worked his way toward the door. It wasn't easy. People had piled their bags and trunks everywhere. With the lights on, it wouldn't have been a problem, but in the darkness, everything was harder.

"Where are you going?" Tock asked him.

Tock slept at the front of the van, right behind the driver's seat. Preston noticed that Tock didn't lower his voice. He didn't care who he woke with his loudness.

"Just to the bathroom."

"Freaking mosquitoes are killing me."

"That's because you're near the door."

"Oh, thanks, genius boy."

Preston didn't reply. He swung past the last mound of bags and nearly stumbled going out the door. Immediately, a warm breeze hit him. The air tasted good, though. It tasted of pine and mist. A small rib of moon hung just above the tree line.

Before he could decide what he was doing outside, he saw something move near the front of the van. He stopped breathing for a moment and tried to make his eyes penetrate the darkness. Whatever it was looked big. Bear-big, maybe, or deer-sized. Small hairs on the back of his neck went up. He took half a step back toward the van door.

"What are you doing out here?" Olivia asked.

She had been the bear. He felt himself relax. He nearly laughed. Big, brave man out in the Minnesota woods.

"Bathroom," he said.

"I couldn't sleep," she said. "It feels claustrophobic inside. It's too stuffy or something."

"Want to make the fire again?"

"Sure," she said. "I'm also starving."

"We don't have anything to eat right now."

"I know. That's a problem, wouldn't you say?"

"It's not a big problem. It's just a bother. We can last."

"I don't think Flash is coming back anytime soon," she said. "I think we're on our own."

It felt nice to talk quietly in the darkness, Preston reflected. It felt natural. Frankly, he didn't care if Flash came back. Not that he wanted Flash to be hurt at all, but he kind of liked being on his own. He liked being responsible for his own choices. He had a sense that maybe Olivia felt the same way.

"I don't mind it," Preston said. "I kind of like it, actually. Is that weird?"

"No, I get what you mean. No adults. It's kind of cool."

"I wouldn't even mind walking out," Preston said. "Just doing it because. Just because. As an adventure."

"We could do it."

"Trouble is, we don't know what comes after the thirty miles. That might just be the end of One Hundred Mile Road."

"We'd run into something sooner or later. It's not forest forever. There are probably camps along the way."

"Walking without eating wouldn't be easy."

"Sooner we start, the better our chances. If we hang out here for a couple days, it's not going to make us stronger."

"You've got a point. But someone's going to come along eventually."

She didn't say anything. When she did speak again, it was about something else. "If Tock starts to work on one of us, let's make a deal that the other will jump in," she said. "You okay with that?"

"You mean like an alliance?"

"Sure. Whatever. He'll be less of a threat if he sees us as united."

"He might be listening," Preston whispered, suddenly realizing the door to the van remained open.

"I don't care. I'd like him to know what's what. I'm sick of him bullying everyone."

"Especially Simon."

She stayed quiet. Then she moved off, and he didn't

know if she had gone into the bushes herself, or if she had gone off to work on the fire. A moment later, he heard her snapping branches.

"Get some pinecones," she said.

Maggie moved closer to the fire. The fire was the best thing around.

Meanwhile, she tried not to listen to the argument. The argument went on and on and on. It started at first light and kept going. It revolved around what to do next. *Go or stay? Leave or hunker down?* She was sick of hearing about it. Personally, she thought it made no sense whatsoever to walk out. It was thirty miles, maybe more, and once they left the shelter of the van, they were committed. The van provided a center. Once they left it, they would be exposed. Everything she knew about survival tactics said stay with the boat, stay with the vehicle, don't leave. Don't let go of the boat and swim for shore, because shore appeared closer than it was in reality and you could drown in the attempt. Cling to the boat.

"It's getting hotter," she said when the conversation paused. "I can smell it."

"You're nuts," Tock said.

"When the cicadas make that noise," she said, "it means it's going to be really hot."

"It's August," Bess said. "It's the hottest August on record."

"I know, I know," Maggie said. "This kind of heat is dangerous. We should be careful about forest fires, too."

"We could use some rain," Olivia said. "We could use it bad."

"Do you think it could reach a hundred?" Preston asked no one in particular. "I think it could. I think it could reach a hundred today."

"It would make walking out pretty hard," Olivia said.

"If we walk ten miles a day, we're out in three days," Tock said. "Ten miles isn't much to walk if you have all day to do it. Even in this heat."

"Humans can walk four miles an hour," Preston said. "I read that once."

"So ten hours of walking will get us out of here. That isn't that bad," Olivia said.

"Could we just go? We're wasting time here," Tock said.

"We're also nearly out of water," Preston said. "We should have a conversation about the water."

"It's a bad idea to leave the van," Maggie said. "This is the only shelter for a long way."

"If we head back to camp," Preston said, "we can at least be sure we'll come to something."

People didn't listen to one another, Maggie realized. They talked *at* one another, but they didn't listen. Everyone had a position, and they defended it as if to relinquish any ground was to lose something. It was called zero-sum thinking, she remembered from a class she had taken with Mr. Gossling, her sixth-grade math teacher. Some people went through their lives believing if they lost, the other person won. Or vice versa.

"We could split up," Maggie said, trying to articulate a position Mr. Gossling might have endorsed. "Some of us could stay, and some could go. Some could go back to camp, and the others could follow the road out. It doesn't have to be only one thing or another."

"It doesn't have to be one thing or another." Tock mocked her with his voice.

"It doesn't," she said. "You're mistaken if you think it can be only one thing or another. It's not binary."

"It's not binary," Tock repeated, making his voice sound idiotic.

Maggie hated when Tock mocked her. She hated it especially because she feared she sounded like his version of her. She realized other people found her annoying, but she wasn't quite sure why they did. Tock was simply the worst example.

"We need to go out for water, anyway," Olivia reasoned. "Why don't we walk a mile or two toward the end of the road and see what it's like? We'll probably cross some water, and we can fill up whatever drinking containers we have. We can make a decision from that point."

"Sounds like a plan, Stan," Tock said. "Let's do it."

"Are we going to pack up everything?" Bess asked. "Should we bring everything?"

No one answered for a time. Then Olivia took charge.

"We're going to walk. Bring what you need. Bring extra clothes – something to shade you from the sun.

We'll make a decision when we reach water whether to go forward or back. How's that sound?"

"Ring-a-ding-ding," Tock said.

That didn't sound like something a kid would say, Maggie thought. That was something Tock's dad probably said. Just thinking of Tock's father and both of them acting like crazy, gung ho Marines with crew cuts and camo pants made Maggie smile. Then she thought of Tock as a little baby, already dressed in camo pants and with a mushroom haircut, and her smile turned into a laugh.

"What, are you going nutso on us?" Tock asked her.

"Let's go!" Olivia said. "We're leaving in ten minutes."

"It's getting hotter," Maggie said again, but she understood no one listened.

SURVIVAL TIP #2

Signaling is often the most overlooked of the basic survival skills. Three fires aligned in a row is an internationally understood distress signal. Use mirrors if you have them to alert passing aircraft to your circumstances. Use rocks or lines of sand to write out "HELP" in large letters. Effective signaling is every bit as important as food or water when it comes to survival, and it often makes the difference between life and death, rescue or continued peril.

CHAPTER 5

Olivia liked being in charge. She liked walking at the head of the group. Each time she turned around to see her ragtag followers, she felt stoked. Not that she was some big deal, she reminded herself. It wasn't like that. But someone needed to make decisions, and for reasons she didn't entirely understand, people listened when she made them. It was like a universal law of some sort: Whoever made a decision with the sharpest focus, with the most authority, inherited the right to make them. *Weird*, she reflected, *but true.*

But the big decision, she knew, hadn't yet arrived. That would arrive as soon as they hit water. Then they would have to commit to moving forward or going back. Good water anyway. They had already crossed a few muddy trickles, but they hadn't yet encountered an honest-to-goodness stream. It wouldn't be long, she figured. It was the land of ten thousand lakes, after all.

The next time she turned around, she saw Tock walking at the edge of the road. He refused to join the group, exactly. He was with them but apart. While everyone else had hurried to get clothes from their luggage and dug around in the van for any water bottles, Tock had concentrated on devising a weapon. Now he wore the van's tire iron through a loop in his belt. It was a heavy, ridiculous-looking thing, but it was formidable, too. Whenever he came to a decent-sized rock, he pulled it out and whacked the metal against the stone. The clang was really starting to grate on Olivia.

She was still thinking about Tock when something remarkable happened.

A moose suddenly appeared on the road. They had seen plenty of moose all summer, but this one simply stepped out of the woods and stopped to look around. It had enormous antlers, but it didn't look full-grown in its body. It looked young, Olivia thought. She watched it tilt its head like a kid shaking water out of his ear. For a long moment, the image of the moose with the green pines behind it made a perfect postcard shot. Then Olivia felt as though someone had taken a long, screechy draw across a violin string, because the moose that had been tranquil a moment before suddenly curled back into itself and slowly became alert. If it had been possible, Olivia could have believed that the moose had gathered its own molecules into a different configuration. It became *more intense* somehow. She couldn't believe that a moose could do such a thing, but it slowly, slowly arched its back and blew air out of its nostrils.

Then, like a train beginning to move inch by inch, then foot by foot, it charged.

Preston ran for the trees. The last thing he observed on the road, the very last thing, was the moose closing in like a missile on Simon. The kid stood staring at the moose, too astonished to move at all. The moose had him lined up directly between its antlers. Simon, Preston realized, was dead meat.

But Preston didn't have time to do a thing except run. He saw Tock running almost beside him, but then he lost track of Tock and of everything except the ground below him and the panting, heaving rush of the moose plowing down the road.

Preston stumbled jumping off the edge of the road and scrambled up as fast as he could. He didn't want to see the moose coming at him, though the truth was he had no idea where the moose might be. He *heard* the moose, however. It rattled everything, every particle of dust or rock, and he heard people screaming. If he had ever thought of anything like this before – a zombie attack, for example, or a werewolf chasing him – he had always imagined himself calm and calculating and shrewd.

But he had never imagined a moose attack. Not in a million years. And he sure wasn't calm.

He scrambled behind a stand of birch trees and quartered around away from the road, hoping if the moose had followed that he could use the trees to shield himself. When he glanced back, he saw the moose, but it was still up on the road, looking around, dazed. Preston tried not to meet the animal's eye. It reminded him of the game he had played as a kid with his cousin Jed.

Big bad wolf, what time is it?

Two o'clock, the wolf – cousin Jed – would answer.

Preston would take a step toward the wolf, then repeat the question.

Big bad wolf, what time is it?

Seven o'clock, the wolf answered.

When the wolf answered *midnight*, everyone had to run back to base. If the wolf got you, you became the wolf.

Now a moose stood in front of him, angled sideways, and Preston watched the long draw of air flare the animal's nostrils. Watching it, Preston realized the temperature had risen. The animal looked coated in sweat, and its nostril blows made it appear shiny and mythical. A ghost moose, Preston thought. A phantom silver moose.

He was glad to have the birch trees between him and the moose. When he glanced to his right, he saw Tock had climbed the first skirt of branches in a spruce tree. *Smart*, he thought. Tock had done a smart thing.

For a long moment or two, nothing happened. The moose remained quiet. Preston deliberately breathed through his mouth. He did not want to do anything that would alert the moose to his location. He didn't even bother squatting down for fear the slightest motion would trigger a charge. He remained still and watched the moose, astonished that this had happened.

It was only after his heart had slowed that he saw the shirt dangling from the moose's left antler.

A shirt, he wondered, not comprehending. It took a moment to make the image real in his mind. It wasn't a shirt anyway. It was a piece of cloth, maybe a piece of backpack, but it dangled from the moose's antler like an absurd earring. Whenever the moose moved its head – something it barely did – the cloth swung like a dull counterweight to its movement. Preston had seen pictures of bullfights in Spain when the picadors had punched their lances into the bull's skin, and the bull had appeared rocky and uncertain. That's what the moose looked like to him.

But what was the cloth dangling from its antler?

Preston squinted and tried to see. The moose pawed at the ground, then bent to eat something. Finally, the moose lifted its head, almost, Preston reflected, like someone emerging from a dream.

The moose took a step forward, seemed to reconsider, then turned directly toward Preston and began walking forward. Preston shrunk down behind the birch trees, thinking it was too late. He looked rapidly around him, wondering what tree he could climb. He saw that Tock had made his way up onto a higher branch and almost ran to join him, but then he thought about the moose trampling him and felt the strength go out of his legs. When Preston looked back, he saw the moose veer off from his line, paralleling the road and heading toward Camp Summertime, finally breaking into a trot that took it away.

Preston did not move.

Not even when the moose was out of sight.

Not even when he heard the screams begin up on the road.

Bess screamed.

She screamed because her nervous system felt overloaded, and she felt if she didn't scream, she would have exploded.

She screamed because Simon stood in the center of the road, entirely unhurt, the moose having missed him by a fraction of an inch.

She screamed because Maggie lay in the middle of the road, her body twisted in an unnatural way.

She screamed because she could close her eyes and see again the moose charging at them, its head lowered, its eyes red and crazed and unholy.

She screamed because she feared the moose would return to finish its job, only something about the moose's posture had changed just before it walked off. Something had settled, like a person shrugging, and the moose had wandered off aimlessly, almost seeming guilty for what it had done.

Bess wanted to move. But she was terrified the moose would return.

"Get over here!" she screamed at Simon. "Now!"

But he didn't move. He stayed in the middle of the road, apparently too traumatized to follow directions.

Bess leaned forward a little from her position behind a maple tree and peered down the road. She couldn't see the moose, but that didn't mean it wasn't nearby. She tried to listen and hear it – it had been tremendously loud, she remembered, like a car throwing up rocks and dirt as it approached – but no sound returned to her.

The moose is on the loose, she thought.

She wasn't certain why that particular refrain went through her head, but it crawled by, worming its way into her thoughts over and over and over.

The moose is on the loose.

Carefully, slowly, she took a step away from the maple tree.

Her body began to shiver, but she couldn't determine if it was the result of some sort of dehydration or fear. Probably both, she figured. Probably a little of everything under the sun.

The moose is on the loose.

"Simon," she said, forcing her voice to remain calm, "please come over here."

But her brother wouldn't move. She took a few steps and went gingerly onto the road. She looked both ways. She saw the moose tracks going off the road, but otherwise the animal had left nothing behind.

Except Maggie, she remembered.

Maggie had been left behind.

"Holy mother of Pete!" Quincy said from somewhere behind her. "Did you see that? Did you *see* that?"

"I saw it," Bess said.

Bess kept her eyes on her brother and on the road.

The moose is on the loose.

"Is Maggie . . ." Quincy asked, but didn't finish his question.

"I don't know," Bess answered. "I don't know anything."

"The moose was crazy," Quincy said. "Did you see it? It looked like it was on fire or something."

"They're in rut," Preston said.

He had suddenly appeared beside her, Bess saw. She noticed he continued to look up and down the road, checking. No one had gone over to see Maggie yet.

"What's *rut*?" Quincy asked.

"Mating season," Preston said. "They get aggressive in the fall. They can become dangerous."

"Can *become* dangerous?" Quincy said. "I guess that's an understatement."

The moose is on the loose, Bess thought again.

She walked over to her brother and took him in her arms. Her brother didn't like to be hugged, she knew, but she didn't care at the moment. He was alive. The moose had passed so close to him that she still couldn't believe it had missed him.

"Why didn't you run?" she whispered into his ear. "Why didn't you move?"

Simon didn't say anything. It took a full hug and a moment of stepping back before she realized what held his attention. His eyes rested on Maggie. His eyes did not leave Maggie.

CHAPTER 6

Tock finished his push-ups and then flipped onto his back for crunches. He didn't like doing crunches as much as push-ups, because push-ups paid off in visible muscles, while crunches, no matter how many you did, usually sharpened muscles that remained under your shirt. It was important to have a fit core, of course, but it wasn't fun to work on it. Nevertheless, he did forty crunches, finishing the last ten by pedaling his legs forward and back, forward and back, while his breath exploded in tiny little bursts.

"Done," he said aloud when he finished.

No one was around. No one would have cared anyway.

He jumped back to his feet. Then he grabbed the tire iron and slid it into his belt. The weight of the iron pulled his belt down over his hip bone, but he didn't care. He liked feeling the heft of the tire iron close by. He liked knowing he could draw it out and defend himself. Not that he would need it with this group of wimps.

He thought about going into the van, but it was too weird in there. Maggie moaned a lot. She was not going to make it, Tock suspected. The moose had seen to that. Maggie wasn't going to get well anytime soon. Not today, not tomorrow, not even if rescue happened to arrive in the next five minutes.

He thought about doing some more push-ups but then decided against it.

He felt hungry. He always felt hungry now, and his stomach made a curling, angry sound that would have been funny if it didn't remind him of how empty he felt.

"Tock, can you come inside the van?" Preston asked from the van stairs after he had wheezed open the door. "We want to talk about what our plan should be."

"Our plan should be to get going."

"We'd like to talk about it. As a group. We need your help."

"We need to go," Tock said, but he went in the side port of the van anyway. Preston shut the van door behind him, as if privacy in a million acres of pines was something to worry about.

Olivia knelt on a bench seat. Someone had cleaned up the van. Or organized it anyway, Tock saw. They had jammed the bags onto a few seats in the back, then left the rows closer to the front empty. It made the environment better, but it still didn't speak to the fact that Maggie was . . . mooseified. She lay on a makeshift bed as far from the door as possible. At least, he realized, she had stopped moaning.

"Okay," Preston said, "everyone's here."

"We need to get going," Tock said. "We can't just wait here."

"Would you hold on for a second?" Olivia said. "Just wait a minute. Everyone's going to get a chance to talk."

So this was the big meeting, Tock realized. They had been chasing their own tails since the van broke down, but now with Maggie injured and maybe dying, they had to come up with a plan. *So be it*, Tock thought. He knew what they needed to do, but he also understood they needed to play it out. He swung down onto a front-bench seat and nearly jabbed the tire iron into his ribs. He had to lift up and slide the tire iron out and rest it across his lap.

"We don't have enough food," Olivia said, and held up her index finger to mark the first fact. "That's number one. Two, we don't know if Flash made it back to camp. Three, it's still blazing hot, and we don't have a dependable source of water. We can make fires, but we have counted and there are twenty-seven matches left. It usually takes a couple of matches to make a fire, so figure we can make maybe six more fires or something. It depends, but the point is we can't make unlimited fires. And three . . . are we on number three?"

No one said anything. Olivia nodded and continued. "Maybe it's four. Whatever," she said. "We need to get help for Maggie. She's in bad shape. That's the big thing."

"We need to send off a party," Tock said. "I've been saying it all along. We're wasting time here."

"Who would go in the party if we sent one off?" Quincy asked.

"I'd go," Tock said.

"Simon and Bess should stay here with Maggie," Preston said. "Quincy, too, if he wants. That leaves Olivia, Tock, and me to go for help."

"Let's go," Tock said, and started to stand.

"Hold on," Olivia said. "Yes, Quincy should probably stay. Three of us could travel pretty fast, I'm betting. We could be out in two or three days."

"You don't know that," Quincy said. "You shouldn't pretend to know that. You shouldn't depend on things you don't know."

"We know the road has to lead someplace, bone-head," Tock said. "Roads don't just wander forever. There's a reason we were going up this road."

"Unless it's a cutoff, I mean," Quincy said from his spot on the bus. "It might lead someplace, but it might just lead to another road, and you might have longer to go than thirty miles. I think you should head back to camp. That way you know you'll get somewhere."

Tock was sick of Quincy's mouth. Guys like Quincy bugged him. They could talk and talk and talk, but when it came to action, they never came through. Tock knew he was the opposite: He was better at doing things than talking about them.

"The moose went that way," Olivia said. "Back to camp. I don't want to run into him again."

"That was a freak thing," Preston said, although his voice didn't sound confident. "There's no way it would happen again. That was just a freak thing."

No one said anything.

"Anyway, do we all agree we should split up?" Olivia asked. "We'll send out a party one way or the other? We won't just stay here and wait?"

Tock looked around. Everyone nodded.

"Let's leave first thing in the morning. First light," Olivia said. "We'll assemble our packs tonight and be ready to go. Is that the plan, then?"

No one answered.

"Which way?" Tock asked.

"Away from camp," Olivia said. "If Flash makes it his

way, then fine. Going the other way doubles our chances of rescue."

At that instant, Maggie began moaning again. Tock stood and pushed the door lever open and jumped back onto One Hundred Mile Road. His tire iron clanged against the door frame, and the sound went off into the forest.

Simon thought the fire was particularly big and particularly bright that night. He had trouble sitting next to it. Sometimes the flames licked toward him, and he could almost believe that they wanted to say something. You never knew. So far, from what he could tell, the campers had not used their time very well. Maggie had definitely used her time poorly, and so had Bess.

Sometimes when the flames came close, he smelled the moose again.

It had come right past him. He had reached to touch it, not sure why, and for an instant the moose seemed to recognize him. The moose had a head like a log. It had ticks on it, too, and it had been in the water not long before it charged, because as it went by, Simon felt moisture.

People talked.

Simon watched the flames.

A little later, Tock and Olivia and Preston brought out their backpacks and began stuffing clothes into them. Simon watched. It was an excellent use of time to both watch the fire and judge their packing skills. Simon enjoyed it. Whenever his attention moved from the backpacks, the moose seemed to be ready to carry off his thoughts. Strange, Simon reflected. He wondered if the reason the moose had trampled Maggie was because he, Simon, had held his hand out to the moose. That was possible, he believed. Charging, the moose seemed to send his eyes over Simon's body – but especially his hand – and then passed within an inch in order to crush Maggie under its hooves.

Maggie had used her time poorly, certainly.

He was still watching them pack their bags when Bess came and sat next to him. She put her head on his shoulder. He wanted to move it away, but he knew it was important to her. His therapist, Ms. Micklejohn, had told him that.

"I'm sorry, Simon," Bess whispered. "I'm sorry I left you out in the road and ran when the moose came."

Simon didn't say anything. He did not know what he was supposed to say. Bess had a different version of things than he did.

"It could have been you instead of Maggie," she said, her voice down by his shoulder. "You could have been killed."

Simon wanted to tell her about the moose, and how it had looked when it charged, and how he had seen ticks on its skin and had smelled its last lake swim, but he couldn't make the words line up.

"Yes," he said.

Ms. Micklejohn had taught him you could always say yes, and often that was enough for people.

"Were you frightened?" Bess asked.

"Yes," he said again.

"I don't blame you. Poor Maggie."

Then he watched Quincy drag a dead piece of pine

from the side of the road and toss it onto the fire. Sparks went up and chattered in the darkness. Simon watched them, trying to connect them with imaginary lines, trying to move his eyes so that the sparks would be rejoined and become fire again.

CHAPTER 7

Quincy resented being left behind. Sort of.

He watched Preston and Olivia and Tock lift their backpacks onto their shoulders and tried to sort out his feelings.

Part of him wanted to go.

Part of him was glad to stay.

What he didn't like was the assumption that he needed to stay. That he *should* stay. It made him feel wimpy. It confirmed in his mind that other people saw him as wimpy.

And maybe he was wimpy. He didn't like thinking about that.

"Follow the yellow brick road," Tock said for the thousandth time.

He said it in a Munchkin voice. It was weird.

"The sun is cooking already," Olivia said, adjusting the straps on her pack. "If the sun stays out, we'll need to get in the shade by midday. And you guys need to do a scouting mission for good water."

"Follow the yellow brick road," Tock said again.

"Would you stop saying that?" Preston asked him.

"Follow the yellow brick road," Tock said, louder.

"We'll be back as soon as we can be," Olivia said. *Like a mom*, Quincy thought. *Like a mom leaving for the night.* "If someone comes, tell them we're staying on the road. We'll just keep walking straight."

Quincy nodded. So did Bess. Quincy didn't know what Simon did, because you could never know what Simon was doing. They all stood watching the three backpackers. Olivia took a moment to adjust the straps again around her shoulders. She had jackets and a sleeping bag piled on her pack, though the pack was too small to support it. The others had sleeping bags, too. They looked like snails, Quincy thought. Like snails heading up the green leg of a plant.

"If you need a fire, make one," Olivia said, finally

finished with her shoulder straps. "There's plenty of fire-starter stuff."

"We got it," Quincy said.

It was annoying to be told what to do. Even by Olivia. She meant well, Quincy understood, but it was still annoying.

"Okay, we're out of here," Olivia said. "If I were you guys, I really would go locate some water. Some good water, I mean."

"Follow the yellow brick road," Tock said.

"Jeez," Preston said, and turned on his heel and began walking.

Quincy watched them go. A little farther up the road, he knew, they would find moose tracks and blood. Bad memories.

"I'm going to check on Maggie," Bess said when the backpackers had walked far enough to disappear around the first bend. They hadn't stopped and waved. Quincy didn't know why, but it bothered him that they hadn't done that. It felt like a bad omen.

"I'll collect wood," Quincy said, coming out of his reverie. "Simon, you want to help me?"

Simon didn't answer. Simon never answered, Quincy knew, except on rare occasions with his sister.

"Okay, then," Quincy said.

He walked down the road the other way, his eyes looking for dead branches, his skin already warming under the sun. Olivia had been right about one thing, he conceded. They needed more water. If they were going to stay for a while, they needed a good water source. Water and fire, he mused. Two opposites, each necessary in its own way.

Preston's feet felt sore, and they had only gone a little over a mile. They had at least thirty miles to go, maybe more, and for the first time, Preston had a keen understanding of what thirty miles felt like.

It felt like sore feet, for one thing. And it felt like a long, long way to walk.

He wanted to say something, to ask how the others felt, but he wouldn't give Tock a chance to mock him. So he remained quiet. And his feet felt raw and sweaty. The pack dug into his shoulders, and he was hungry. Very hungry. What had seemed like a good idea back at the van, almost a fun adventure, now felt like a more significant undertaking.

"How's everyone doing?" Olivia asked.

"Follow the yellow brick road," Tock said.

"Thanks," Olivia said. "How about you, Preston?"

"I'm okay," he said.

"My feet hurt on these rocks," Olivia said. "Sneakers don't cut it in this stuff."

"Mine, too," Preston said.

"Follow the yellow brick road," Tock said.

"Are you trying to make this harder?" Olivia asked Tock. "I mean, do you have to work at it, or does it just come naturally?"

"Follow the yellow brick road," Tock said.

Olivia shook her head. She yanked on her shoulder straps again and kept walking. Nothing had changed. The landscape didn't really change, either, Preston observed. *Trees, road, sky, trees, road, sky.* Now and then, they seemed to come to a slight rise or depression in the road, but it was never substantial. The road continued like a straight shot through the green woods. Occasionally, the dirt had furrows or ribs down the center where the road had been eroded. But otherwise, it was simply a straight dirt road.

"Does the camp own all this land?" Preston asked, mostly to make conversation.

"I guess so," Olivia said. "Isn't that what Flash said?"

"I don't really know what Flash said. I could never understand the guy. He mumbled too much."

Olivia smiled.

"He *was* hard to understand," she agreed. "He always talked through his teeth or something."

"He should have made it to camp by now," Preston said.

Tock snorted.

"What?" Preston asked.

"He didn't make it to camp, you dope," Tock said. "If he had made it to camp, we would be on a bus out of here by now."

"Then what do you think happened to him?" Olivia asked. "If you know so much, tell us, oh wise one."

Tock made a sharp screeching sound with his tongue and lips and drew his thumb across his throat.

"No way," Olivia said.

"Okay, wait and see," Tock said.

"I hope not," Preston said. "He wasn't a bad guy."

The conversation made Preston feel squirrely in his stomach. He didn't like imagining Flash alone in the woods. Or worse. It bugged him to hear Tock be so casual about it. Besides, they were now in the woods, too, trying to pull off exactly what Flash had tried to pull off. If something bad had happened to Flash, it could happen to them, too. He didn't like thinking that.

"How are we going to sleep tonight?" he asked, to change the subject. "We're going to need some sort of shelter."

"We'll make a debris hut," Tock said. "No worries."

"What's a *debris hut*?" Olivia asked.

"You'll see," Tock said. "I've got skills."

"It's going to be buggy," Preston said.

"We'll be okay," Olivia said. "I want to see this debris hut. Where'd you learn about it?"

Tock shrugged.

"Come on, Tock, tell us," Olivia said. "Be normal for a second."

"My uncle," he said. "He's a big survival guy. You know. That kind of guy."

"You mean like he could go into the woods and live off the land?" Preston asked.

Tock nodded. And he blushed. Preston couldn't believe Tock had revealed a human emotion. For the first time, Preston realized that maybe Tock was a little embarrassed by his background. Maybe it wasn't all gung ho Marine. It was hard to know about Tock. Preston had never met anyone like him.

"Sometimes he took me out and showed me stuff," Tock said. "He lived for a year in a national park in Tennessee, and no one knew about it. He fished and hunted and sometimes he ate food out of the Dumpsters. I know that sounds gross, but people throw away a ton of food. That's what he said, anyway."

"That is so disgusting," Olivia said.

Preston saw the remark hit a soft spot in Tock. He closed down. Preston could see it happen. Suddenly, Preston realized that maybe Tock got hit by peoples' comments more than he might have guessed. It was a vicious cycle. Tock said something stupid, then people responded, then Tock pulled further into his shell. It was strange to realize Tock was human.

"Anyway, Tock," Preston said, covering for Tock, "we're lucky to have you."

"Follow the yellow brick road," Tock said, veering off to the side of the road.

Olivia hoisted her pack higher on her back. Preston tried to keep his mind off his feet. He was still thinking about his toes and about the weight on his shoulders when Olivia stopped. When he looked up, he realized she had stopped because they had come to a fork in the road.

Veer left or veer right? Both roads looked about the same. Maybe the road that went to the left looked a little less traveled, but even that was hard to say for certain.

"Uh-oh," Olivia said.

"Now it gets interesting," Tock said.

"There's probably a sign somewhere along here," Preston said.

"Maybe," Olivia said. "And maybe not."

"What's the plan?" Preston asked.

"I'll go down this road a little and look for signs," Olivia said, pointing to the left. "You guys go down the other road. Yell if you see anything. Don't go too far. We'll meet back here in five minutes."

"Whatever you say, boss," Tock said.

"Five minutes," Olivia repeated. "Shout if you see anything."

"Follow the yellow brick road," Preston said.

Tock laughed. Then he walked off on the road that veered right. Preston followed him.

Bess lit the seventh match and held it to the birch bark. *Seven matches*, she thought as she carefully moved the fire onto the birch. The birch crumpled and began shivering with light. She brought another piece of birch bark into the tiny flame and waited for it to catch. The birch bark flared suddenly, and she dropped it before she had it properly positioned. It lay on its side, burning but not contributing its heat to the pile of twigs she had built next to it.

"I hate this," she said under her breath.

Quincy didn't say anything. Neither did Simon. They both squatted next to the fire pit like two frozen gargoyles.

She didn't know how it had become her problem to start a fire, but it had. It was getting late in the afternoon, and they needed a fire for security and for the pleasure it brought.

But they had gone through seven matches. *She* had gone through seven matches, she amended. That wasn't good. They could not continue to use so many matches to get a fire started.

"That's better," she whispered when the twigs finally caught and the fire began burning more brightly. She fed tiny twigs into the yellow wedge of flame. The smoke smelled like pine and something damp, something like basements. But it was still a good scent. She rocked back a little on her knees and watched the flame continue to grow.

"That should do it," Quincy said.

"Just feed it carefully," Bess said. "You can't rush a fire."

"Birch bark works."

"Yes, but it flashes up and has to go to something. That's the trick. You have to transfer it to a pile of tinder."

Quincy held out his hands to the flames. The air above the road became foggy and dense. You could see a dull reflection of the fire in the muggy haze.

Still, it was better outside than it was inside the van. Maggie was inside the van. And Maggie was drifting away. It was harder and harder to be near her.

"I'm starving," Quincy said.

"We're all starving," Bess said. "We can eat a little in a while."

"They took almost all of it," Quincy said.

"They're going to need it. They're burning more calories than we are."

Quincy shrugged. He leaned forward and put more wood on the fire. It was a little too much wood, Bess noted, but she didn't say anything. She knew she could be bossy at times. She felt she had been bossy a lot with Quincy.

"How are you doing, Simon?" she asked her brother.

She didn't expect an answer, and he didn't give her one. It still made sense to check in with him. Sometimes she felt like he was a balloon dangling way above her on a string. Sometimes you had to look up and make sure it was still there.

"So they've walked a day," Quincy said. "Two more days and they should be out."

"If everything goes okay."

"Why wouldn't it?" he asked.

"You want a million reasons or just one or two?"

"They'll do okay."

"Maybe they will, maybe they won't," she said. "They should have gone back toward Camp Summertime. That way they would have known where they were going. They would have had a destination."

"I guess they thought Flash went that direction. Isn't that what Olivia said? Plus, the moose is that way."

"We can't spend the rest of our lives being frightened of a moose."

"It did a pretty good job on Maggie. You have to admit that," he said, making the obvious point.

Quincy put more wood on the fire. It was too much. Bess reached in quickly and pulled out a few of the stoutest branches. The fire needed air more than fuel at this stage.

"Easy," she said.

"It would have caught."

"Maybe. And maybe it would have gone out. Just take it slow. There's no rush. We have all night."

"We could head back toward camp," Quincy said. "We don't have to stay here. We can make our own decision about what to do."

"We have Maggie."

Quincy shrugged. Bess knew what the shrug meant. It wasn't good.

"We have to do what we can for her," Bess said.

"I know."

"That moose is long gone by now."

"Probably," he agreed.

"I couldn't believe it. Could you? Could you actually believe what was happening?"

"Not really."

"It all happened like a movie," Bess said, closing her eyes and remembering. "It seemed like we were going to stand up, dust the popcorn off our laps, then go to bed or something. I never expected it to be real."

"It was real, but I know what you mean."

"And Maggie . . . she looked fake somehow. Like it couldn't really be happening to her. It was like a nightmare, only it was more real than a nightmare could ever be. It was just so vivid or something."

Quincy nodded. She glanced at Simon. Whatever he thought about the moose attack, he wasn't saying. At times she wondered what it would be like to have a brother who talked and laughed and did what brothers usually did. Sometimes it made her jealous to know other girls had nice brothers, easy brothers, brothers who could help their sisters out. Not Simon. It was always a one-way street with Simon, though it was mean to think it.

She was glad when Quincy spoke again and got her out of her thoughts.

"So we just wait?" Quincy asked after a little while, shifting down into a cross-legged position. "We just make fires and wait?"

"What else do you want to do?"

Quincy shrugged. But Bess knew what he was feeling. She felt restless, too. She wanted to do something, anything, but they couldn't. Not yet. If Maggie went away for good, then yes, yes they could do something. But not now. Maybe not for a while. Maggie still had rights.

"I bet there's stuff to eat around here that we don't even know about it. Natural foods or something," Quincy said, looking around. "There's probably tons to eat right near here, but we just don't have that knowledge."

"Probably so."

"We're smart, but we're dumb."

"I know what you mean."

"What are you going to eat first thing?" he asked.

"I'm going to take a shower first thing."

"Okay, but afterward."

"Something good. I don't know."

"I want a hamburger," he said, his voice filled with longing. "Or maybe a club sandwich. I love club sandwiches. With an ice-cold Coke. I want the slushy kind of ice. And fries on the side."

"But first a shower."

"I want a shower, but I want to eat first."

"Mashed potatoes," Simon said.

Bess looked at her brother. So did Quincy. Then their eyes came together, and they started to laugh. Bess had seen her brother enter a conversation before in a similar way, but never with such perfect timing. It made her laugh harder to think about mashed potatoes. Who wanted mashed potatoes more than any other food? Only her brother would want that.

"Mashed potatoes," Quincy said, still laughing. "That's what you want, Simon? Out of all the food in the world, you want potatoes smashed up."

"They do sound good," Bess said.

"You like mashed potatoes?" Quincy asked her brother. "I like them, too, but only when they're good and fluffy."

"They're the best when they're a little hard," Bess said.

"Okay, so a shower for Bess, a club sandwich for me, and mashed potatoes for Simon. We should be able to do that."

Bess put more wood on the fire. Then she stood and said she was going to go in and check on Maggie.

"Okay," Quincy said.

"I'll be right back," she told Simon.

He didn't move. He liked the fires, she knew. They mesmerized him.

Later, she would say she knew the minute she stepped in the van. She *knew*. Whether that was true or not, by the time she made it three-quarters of the way down the aisle, she knew Maggie was gone. To her surprise, she didn't panic. She didn't call out to Quincy or Simon or do very much of anything. She simply walked forward, took Maggie's wrist to check for a pulse, then bent over and put her ear next to Maggie's mouth. No air. No breath. Her pulse did not exist.

Bess dropped Maggie's hand, then thought better of it and folded Maggie's hand on her chest. She pulled the sweatshirt that had covered her up over her face. Then she took a deep breath, felt it shudder in her chest, and slowly turned and walked back to the fire.

CHAPTER 8

It looked like a haunted house, Olivia thought.

She stood in the middle of the path and studied the structure that had slowly emerged from the woods. A greasy, muggy fog covered it. And vines or moss or something green and foul smothered it. Her backpack felt like it wanted to yank her away, and she actually took a step back but then stopped, fascinated, unable to resist the temptation.

Like a haunted house, she thought again.

Or worse. Like a zombie hotel. Like the kind of place where kids go to camp on the weekend, then some sort of evil creature, man or beast, begins skulking around and picking them off one by one. And the entire time, the kids are unaware of what's happening until it becomes ridiculously apparent that something totally bad is creeping around, but by then it's too late. Then they start kicking off in all sorts of unusual places, and eventually the girl or guy opens a closet door and the audience sees that someone is hanging from the back of the door and is in all kinds of trouble, but the character in the haunted house doesn't see it, and the audience watches with dread while the body begins slowly *movingggggg*. The audience begins edging forward and letting a scream slowly work its way up from the belly, and then the body on the back of the door begins reaching out and . . .

That kind of place, Olivia thought. She shook herself. Her eyes traveled carefully over the building. The house was what her cousin Donna – who was in real estate in Duluth – would have called a Painted Lady. A Victorian. A wedding cake of a house.

Big wraparound porch. Dormers and turrets. Once upon a time it was white, but now it simply appeared moss-colored. Broken windows. Broken balusters on the porch so that the whole thing resembled a face with shattered teeth.

And it smiled.

Come on in, it invited. *Come on in and stay awhile.*

I should yell for the guys, she thought. *I should yell right now.*

But she didn't. She couldn't really say why she didn't, but she didn't. That was that.

At the same time, she became aware of how alone she felt. How isolated. The house had a sucking feeling, as though you couldn't resist it even though you knew you should. A chain on what looked to be an old post for a dog clinked a little in the late-afternoon breeze. For a blink of her eyes or two, she had a sense of what this house must have looked like back in the day. It wasn't a cheap house, she didn't think. It was a decent house in its time, maybe even a great house. She wondered why she had never heard of it before. She wondered why no one had ever mentioned it at the camp. It should have been a landmark.

She was still looking at the house when Tock snuck up behind her, jabbed his thumbs into her ribs, and nearly stopped her heart.

"Jeez! Tock, you could have frightened me to death! Don't ever do that to me again!" she yelled.

She stamped around in a small circle as if she wanted to be rid of a swarm of spiders crawling over her legs.

Tock laughed. So did Preston.

Eventually, she gained control of herself. She was pretty sure she must have looked ridiculous stamping around like that. She hated Tock in that moment; she hated them both.

"Wow, that is a creepy place," Preston said. "Seriously creepy."

"Let's go inside," Tock said. "That place is awesome!"

"I am not going inside that house! That house wants you to come inside," Olivia said, slowly shaking off the residue of her earlier feeling. "Can't you feel that?"

"Ghost hotel," Tock said, obviously enjoying himself. "There might be some food in there."

"There's no food in there!" Olivia said. "Are you insane? Why would there be food in there?"

"Could be canned stuff. You don't know for sure."

"We could spend the night there," Preston said. "At least it would be inside."

"You are completely insane now," Olivia said. "Am I the only one who thinks that place is seriously haunted?"

She looked at them, but they were being boys. They were daring each other; she could tell. It's what boys did. And Tock, being Tock, ratcheted everything up whenever he could. Preston had to go along with it. That's just the way it was.

"I'm in," Tock said. "I am so in."

"Me, too," Preston said. "Besides, there could be a phone. There could be something."

It was so absurd that Olivia didn't bother to respond. She looked long and hard at the balusters, the grin the house had along the front porch. It was too weird.

"You have to promise me that you'll evaluate it honestly," she said. "Objectively. Okay? Do you promise?"

Tock nodded. So did Preston. Then Tock pulled the tire iron out of his belt and started toward the house. They were going in, she realized. It was the stupidest idea on earth, but at that moment, it hardly mattered. She was outvoted.

And besides, she wanted to see inside the house, too. It was weird, but she did.

Δ   Δ   Δ

"Now what?" Quincy asked.

He looked at the van. They had both been looking at the van for a long time. First, they would look at the fire, then at Simon, then at the van. It was as if they expected something to change when they knew perfectly well nothing was going to change. Maggie was finished changing. They knew it in their heads, he realized, but they didn't know it in their hearts yet.

"We start walking tomorrow," Bess said. "We go back to Camp Summertime."

"Someone is bound to show up. Maybe we should wait."

"We can't wait forever. Olivia was right about that. So was Tock."

"It's weird, though," Quincy couldn't help saying. "The whole thing."

"I'm not sleeping in the van," Bess said. "I'm going to keep the fire going and sleep out here."

"It will be too hot when the sun starts to rise."

"I don't care," Bess said. "You didn't see her."

"It's just Maggie."

Bess nodded. But she didn't say anything.

"The moose is back that way," he said.

She shrugged.

Quincy stood and put some more wood on the fire. They had a fair supply of fuel. They had enough water temporarily, but they had to find some the next day. As soon as they had discovered Maggie's condition, her final condition, they had collected wood like crazy people. Now it was getting dark and foggy. The fog rolled in over the road like a creature slowly sniffing its way into a clearing. Quincy had never been so aware of the fog. The flames from the fire looked especially yellow against it. It was almost pretty if you could step back and forget why you were sitting beside the fire in the first place.

"Let's leave first thing in the morning," Bess said. "That's what I recommend."

"We'll have to spend at least two nights out."

"We can do that. We'll build really big fires. Nothing will bother us, if that's what you're worried about. The moose isn't a threat."

"If we can't start a fire, we'll be in real trouble."

"So what's your plan?" Bess asked.

"I don't have a plan. Not really."

"Look, we don't know what's happening to those other guys. To Tock's group. And we don't know what happened to Flash. So we can either sit around and hope someone comes – and deal with Maggie – or we can make a plan and stick to it. I vote we hike back to camp."

"I wasn't saying no," Quincy said, feeling a little under attack. "I was just pointing things out."

"I'd leave right now if we could. If it weren't dark."

Then, suddenly, Quincy heard a wolf howl. At least he thought it was a wolf howl. It came low and mournful, rising slowly as though it had seeped out of the ground. It was an amazing sound, one that tickled his ears. Then another howl met the first one and he realized, yes, these really were wolves and he really was hearing them.

"Are those . . ." Bess started in a low voice, but Simon cut her off.

"Wolves," Simon said.

Simon stood and cocked his head in the wolves' direction. It was the most engaged Quincy had ever seen Simon. He was *on* those wolves.

"And you're sure they're not coyotes?" Bess asked.

But Quincy was sure. And he was sure Bess was sure. And Simon was definitely, positively sure. You couldn't mistake that sound if you tried.

"Wolves," Simon said.

"I think so, too," Quincy said.

"There are wolves in Minnesota," Bess said, her voice quiet and firm. "We have a good population of wolves in Minnesota."

"Coyotes have a higher pitch," Quincy said. "They sound like they're gargling. Wolves sound lonely and like the forest would sound if it could speak."

Then no one said anything for a while. The wolves howled again, this time with four or five voices blended. It was beautiful, Quincy thought, but also terrifying. He knew a little bit about wolves from Mr. Fitzsimmons's biology class, knew they didn't randomly attack humans, knew they were social animals that used cooperation to hunt. They hunted elk and deer and moose, not humans, but the sound of them went down into his bones somewhere. It was an old sound, he decided. A really old sound.

"You like the wolves, Simon?" Bess asked her brother when the wolves finished. "You've never heard one, have you?"

Simon shook his head. He slowly lowered himself next to the fire again. Quincy didn't know how, but he could feel the wolves weren't going to howl again. They had moved away. The woods around them felt empty again. Simon seemed to sense it, too.

"As long as we keep a fire going, we'll be okay," Bess said as she put more wood onto the fire. "Walking back to camp, I mean."

"How many matches do we have left?"

"The other guys took fifteen," Bess said. "That left us twelve. I used seven for this fire."

"So we have five matches left?"

"If you can do better, then go ahead," Bess said. "Be my guest."

"I didn't say that," Quincy said, seeing for a second how touchy Bess could be. "I'm just trying to understand everything. I want to know what we have."

"If we're careful, we can do better."

"If it rains, though, we'd be in trouble."

"We'll bring a lot of paper," Bess said. "We can do it."

Quincy nodded. It felt hard to make decisions without all the information. You had to consider a million different factors. Part of him liked it, though. It was like a word problem you got in math, only this word problem was real. *If Simon and Bess and Quincy left a stranded camp van in the Minnesota woods with five matches left, and they had not eaten anything solid in X days, then what was the likely outcome of their adventure?*

It was better than any math problem he could remember.

"Let's go for it," he said. "First thing in the morning. First light."

"Simon, you in?" Bess asked her brother.

Simon didn't do anything but look at the fire.

"Mashed potatoes," Quincy said, knowing it was lame even as he said it. "If we get back, we get mashed potatoes."

Then the fog rolled over the road, and he tasted moisture on his tongue and felt it on his hands and in his hair.

Δ   Δ   Δ

Preston didn't like the house.

He also felt it didn't like him.

And that was purely strange. As he walked up the first two steps – the third was rotted, and he could look down at the ground beneath it – he wondered why they were going to investigate it. The road clearly went the other direction. That had been easily established after all, and they had come back quickly, double-timing it, to get Olivia and tell her what they had discovered.

But she had discovered something of her own. She had discovered the house.

"This is freaky," Preston said, pronouncing each word separately and distinctly so there could be no mistaking the weirdness.

"Guys . . ." Olivia said, but she didn't finish her thought.

"It's awesome," Tock said, stepping high to pass over the third step. He poked at the open space with his tire iron. "This is where the hand shoots up and grabs the first kid and drags him down to the basement."

"Or her," Olivia said.

"Or her," Preston agreed.

"This house is horrible," Olivia said. "I swear, it's grinning at me."

"It feels like that, doesn't it?" Preston asked. "What's a house doing out here, anyway? I thought the camp owned all the land for miles around."

"This was probably here when they bought it," Tock said. "It was probably in bad shape even then."

Preston noted that Tock paused before stepping onto the porch. Big, brave Tock still got the jimjams just like anyone else. It made Preston smile to see it, though he suspected his smile looked more like a grimace. He stepped over the big gap in the stairs and scrambled up next to Tock. Olivia stood on the downslope side of the opening.

"There's something down there," she said, pointing. "Down where the step should be."

"You're flipping," Tock said.

"I swear," Olivia said. "Something white. It looks like bones. I'm not kidding."

"That's just freaky," Preston said.

He leaned away from the top stair to see into the space. Olivia pointed a little to the left, and he saw what she had seen. It looked like a rib cage, a cat's rib cage maybe, or a squirrel's. He didn't see a skull, but he saw what looked like arms extended forward, almost as though the animal had died mid-stride. Maybe someone threw a cat's bones down there. Or some animals had dragged it there. It was hard to guess.

"Let's get inside," Tock said, pulling back from where he had been looking down through the stairs, too. "They're just some old bones."

"You don't find it a little creepy that we have to cross over some old bones just to get in the house?" Olivia asked.

"Whatever," Tock said. "Things happen."

Olivia took the big step over the open area. She climbed up onto the porch and turned around to look at them. "This is a bad idea," she said.

Tock wiggled his eyebrows. He slapped his tire iron against his hand. Then he took a few steps and tapped the tire iron on the door. It made a loud, hollow sound. He whacked it hard.

"Hello!" Tock called in a singsong voice. "We're here! You have visitors!"

"You'd freak fast enough if someone opened the door," Olivia said. "I guarantee it."

"We all would," Preston said.

He felt like his nerves wanted to jangle through his skin. To add to the creepiness of the house, the sun had disappeared. They were in twilight. Maybe post-twilight. It was going to be dark inside the house in no time. He tried to remember the phase of the moon, but he couldn't make himself think clearly. Usually he knew something like that.

Tock pushed the door. It fell open without any protest. It didn't make a groaning sound or squeal on its hinges, Preston realized. It opened happily, almost too easily. That simple fact bothered him more than anything else that had happened so far regarding the house.

It welcomed us inside, he thought.

Olivia had been correct about that.

"Awesome," Tock said again, and crossed the threshold.

Inside, it looked like a birthday cake that had been left out in the rain and had started to melt. That's what Preston thought. The room directly beyond the door was not a room at all, really, but a hallway. Down the hallway, a set of dark stairs ran up to the second floor. The stairs looked to be in reasonable shape; no broken steps that he could see, no broken banisters. Off the hallway on the left was some sort of sitting room. A fireplace had collapsed on itself and broken into bricks and stones that had crushed the mantel and taken part of the wall with it. Preston saw the last of the twilight through a large crack in the wall. It wasn't a room anyone wanted to enter.

On the other side of the hallway, he saw what must have been the dining room back in the day. A built-in china cabinet had taken up one side of the room toward the back of the house, but it had been partially demolished by someone years before. Glass and wood lay scattered across the floor. Kids had come in and written their initials with spray paint. The remnants of an inner tube – the kind you'd float in on a hot day – lay shredded in the corner.

All the windows were broken. Every last one.

"Okay, we went in the house, and it is in horrible shape," Olivia said. "We've proven we're big and brave. Now can we leave?"

"We need to check the kitchen," Tock said. "We need to check for food."

"You don't want to eat anything from this house," Olivia said.

"You never know until you know," Tock answered.

"Yes, you do. I know right now that I won't eat anything from this house. Preston? What do you think?"

"We're here. We might as well check. And I'm hungry. We need to eat soon no matter what we do."

But it was getting dark. The house felt heavy. It felt heavier and heavier as the darkness moved inside. Preston hated looking at the staircase in front of them. Maybe it tapped into a nightmare – he couldn't quite say – but something about the stairs, the darkness of the wood, the fact that it was still in good condition, made him queasy.

Like it wants us to come upstairs, he thought. *Like it's holding out a hand.*

"The kitchen has to be back there," Tock said, pushing his chin in the direction of the rear of the house. "Down the hallway."

"I hate what we're doing," Olivia said. "Can't you feel it's not right?"

"Let's do it and get going," Preston said. "Let's check and keep moving."

"We could camp in here tonight," Tock said. "It would be drier than outside."

"I am not sleeping in here," Olivia said. "This is not a good place to be."

"You're free to leave," Tock said. "No one said you had to come inside."

Which was, Preston conceded, technically true. Olivia's personality was strong enough to resist anything. But it wasn't realistic to expect her to hang around outside the house while they explored inside. No one wanted to be alone. Not after what happened to Maggie. Not on One Hundred Mile Road.

Tock held out his tire iron and started down the hallway. Little by little, Preston understood that to go into the area that was most likely the kitchen meant they had to pass by the staircase. Had to brush past it and look up the stairs. They had to see the darkness above the steps and see whatever it was that wanted to come down the stairs toward them. He had trouble swallowing thinking about the darkness on the second floor.

That's where whatever lives here is hiding, he thought. *Upstairs, waiting.*

And that's when they heard the footsteps.

CHAPTER 9

What was that?" Olivia asked, her voice like a hiss. "What exactly was that?"

Tock didn't know. His mind had suddenly flushed white and empty. He lifted the tire iron in front of him like a samurai sword and stood ready to combat whatever came at them.

"That sounded like . . ." Preston whispered.

Tock cut him off. "Those were human steps," he said. Because they were. He would have bet money on it.

"Okay, we're going to go into the kitchen to check for food and then we'll go straight out. Everyone on board with that?" Tock asked.

No one answered, so he figured they were.

He turned and went quickly down the remainder of the hallway. His ears strained to hear whatever had made the footsteps, but they had stopped. For now. They had been quick and soft, like someone moving without wanting to be heard. It was a little freaky, Tock admitted to himself.

"Let's go," he said when they arrived at what he took to be the kitchen door. "Ready?"

"You first," Olivia said.

He kicked open the door.

And something ran at him.

It happened so fast that he didn't have a chance to react. It was on him, just like that, just like nothing. He swung his tire iron at whatever it was, but the tire iron bounced on the doorjamb and clanged out of his hand. He screamed, and it was a timid, babyish scream that immediately embarrassed him. But whatever it was – it was too dark to make out anything clearly – kept whining and hissing and sputtering down by his legs.

"Get it off me!" he yelled. "Get it off me!"

He felt Olivia slide next to him and kick at something with all her might.

"Run!" she yelled. "Close the door on it and run!"

Tock fell outside the door and came up onto his feet as fast as he could. He saw Preston scrambling down the hallway, running like a spider monkey, all wild and apish. Tock took off after him. He heard Olivia behind him.

And he heard *it*, the thing in the kitchen, coming after them all.

"Go, go, go, go," he said.

He felt crazy scared. He felt as though he could run through a wall.

But when he came through the front door onto the porch and began to run down the steps, he realized in that last instant that he had forgotten about the missing step.

First he felt air under his foot. Under his left foot. His right foot pushed off from the porch, and he had gone down so many stairs – had leaped down a million of them – that he had entirely forgotten that this set of steps lacked a single riser. So his right foot went down, and the rest of his body weight surged awkwardly to that side. His left foot found nothing to support it, so he fell and careered to port, and he felt himself going down. He heard a snap and realized something had broken, some part of him had broken, and he screamed again, for the second time, he realized. *What a baby*, he thought, even though the pain that surged through his body felt like an electric bolt. Something jabbed into his palm and he felt bewildered to realize he had gone down, lost height, and now stood up to his waist in the middle of the staircase.

Olivia jumped past him. Her knee clipped the side of his head and made her spin and fall, but she landed down at the bottom of the steps. He heard her give a soft *ompph* as air went out of her.

"It was a raccoon!" Preston yelled, his voice mixed up with laughter and fright and a dozen other things Tock couldn't recognize. Preston jumped up and down, giddy, Tock understood, because Preston had gotten away from the danger and felt good about it.

"My leg," Tock said.

He didn't know what else to say about the leg. He didn't want to look down at it. This was bad, he knew. This was really bad.

Olivia stood up. She had had the wind knocked out of her. She bent over and put her hands on her knees.

"It was a raccoon," she said between breaths. "In the kitchen. It came at you."

"Tock?" Preston asked.

"My leg," Tock said. "I think it's broken."

"A freaking raccoon," Olivia said.

She stood straight up slowly. Tock watched her. He didn't know why, but it almost felt as though she had won something and he had lost. He didn't like thinking about it.

"Let's get you out of there before something pulls you down into the basement," she said. "Preston, give me a hand."

"Let's go. I can't sleep, anyway. Let's just get going," Quincy said.

He felt clammy. And uncomfortable. And antsy. He knew Bess hadn't slept much. He had listened to her through the night turning around trying to find a way to sleep, getting up and adding more wood to the fire. He couldn't tell about Simon, but once during the night, when an owl had begun calling nearby – *who cooks for you, who cooks for you*, the owl asked – Simon had sat up and looked a long time in the owl's direction. Who knew what that meant? Quincy had once heard that if an owl called your name, you were doomed, but he doubted Simon had that on his mind.

"It's not even light yet," Bess said.

"It's going to be soon. You can see it getting pale over in the east."

"Suddenly you're a Boy Scout?" Bess asked.

"I've camped," Quincy said. "I just don't make a big deal out of it like some people."

"You go, Quincy," Bess said.

She sat up and stretched. She chucked a few pieces of wood on the fire. It didn't catch right away, but she fanned a flip-flop at it and that helped. Pretty soon the fire ticked along just fine. Quincy moved closer. It felt like his muscles had frozen from stiffness during the night. His hands felt sticky from all the pine pitch.

"Once we leave, there's no turning back," Bess said.

"It isn't that far."

"Flash said thirty miles each way. We're dead center from nowhere."

"Are you having second thoughts?"

"No, not really," Bess said. "I'm realizing that when we leave, we leave. The van gives us some shelter."

Quincy didn't bring up the obvious obstacle of Maggie. Maggie had the van. They didn't.

"Sooner we leave, sooner we get there," Bess said. "We need plenty of paper, and we can't forget the matches. The sleeping bags, too. And bring a change of clothes. Mostly we need water."

Quincy stood. He felt better with a plan. He told himself to quit worrying whether it was the right thing or not. Just do what was ahead of him. That was his plan. Do the next thing, then the next thing, then the next thing. Just keep doing things and pretty soon you'll be back at camp. That's what he told himself.

"I wouldn't be surprised if Flash came along with a car this morning," Bess said, stuffing her sleeping gear into its sack. "That moose freaked us out, and I'm not saying it shouldn't have, but we're not in as much trouble as we might think. Thirty miles won't be easy, but it's flat road and well marked. It could be a lot worse."

Quincy didn't say anything, but he wondered if she was simply talking to psych herself up. If you took a step back, things couldn't be much worse. He didn't see the point in trying to jolly things up. Still, he understood what she was saying and why, and he made a decision to stay positive no matter what, no matter how hard it became.

"Simon, time to wake up!" Bess said. "We have some walking to do."

Simon slowly rolled over. He stared at the fire.

"Up and at 'em, lazybones," Bess said, finishing with her sleeping bag and looking around for more items to jam in her pack. "Help us pack up. You're going to have to carry a pack, too."

Bit by bit, Simon sat up. He held his hands out to the fire. Quincy took a couple more hunks of wood and threw them on the center coals. It didn't make any sense to conserve fuel at this point. He looked toward the east and saw it had become slightly lighter. *Time to go*, he thought. *Time to walk*.

"I don't think your leg is broken," Olivia said. "I know you heard something, but I can't feel any break. Maybe it was something else that made the sound you heard."

"I'm telling you, I heard it break," Tock said. "And it's killing me."

Olivia shrugged. She felt worn out. Preston had felt the leg, too, and he couldn't find anything. Not that any of them were doctors, obviously, but she was fairly certain if something had been broken there would probably be a bunch of swelling. Her entire body of knowledge came from a three-hour first-aid class she had taken at camp. *So be it*, she thought. So far, she couldn't detect any inflammation, although she would have been the first to admit the light wasn't any good. There was no light, in fact, just starlight and whatever illumination they could get from the fire.

They had camped at the *V* where the two roads separated. Preston had insisted on it in case a vehicle came by. They had lugged Tock between them, one of his arms around each of their shoulders, and they had made him as comfortable as possible. He remained in a ton of pain. Olivia could not do a thing for him, she knew, other than make him generally comfortable. He lay against his backpack, his leg on a second backpack – hers – to elevate it.

"We have some decisions to make," Preston said. "We need to decide whether we should go back to the bus or keep going."

"I can't walk," Tock said.

"We'll test it in the morning," Olivia said.

"I'm getting really peeved no one believes my leg is broken when I say that it is."

"No one is saying it isn't," Olivia said. "We're saying we don't know. We're saying the break isn't obvious."

Tock didn't say anything else. Olivia went to get wood. Light had started to appear in the east. She heard thunder, too. It was far off, just a remote rumble, and she hoped it wasn't headed their way.

She grabbed a bunch of dry pine. That, at least, was not a problem. They had more wood than they could burn in a lifetime. She had broken off three lengths of crackle pine, stamping on each one with a satisfying crunch, when suddenly she stopped and let a brainstorm hit her.

It was a brain*storm*, too. A true brainstorm.

It went like this: *Why did the house exist at the end of the road?*

The answer was so easy it almost struck her as too obvious.

A house like this would probably be near a lake.

Land of ten thousand lakes, she told herself.

Right? she asked herself. *Isn't that right?*

They had built the house on a body of water! Of course. Why else would you build a house way out in the woods? And how did the kids who had spray-painted their names on the dining room walls make it to the house? Didn't Flash say the road was gated on both ends? For kids to get in, they had to come over land.

Or across water.

"Guys!" she called, and snatched up the wood and started back. "I just had a brainstorm!"

"Terrific," Tock said.

"Why is that old house built where it is?"

Preston looked at her.

Tock shook his head.

"I'm not going back to that house and the rabid raccoon," Tock said.

"They build houses like that on the water!" she said, dropping the wood beside the fire. "Why else would that house exist where it does? Think about it! We took the road down from camp, then across ... we're going around a lake, don't you see? I remember seeing little flashes of it when we were driving."

"Our lake? The camp lake?" Preston asked.

"Probably not. It's probably another lake. But the kids who spray-painted the house had to get here somehow, and you can bet they didn't drive down the road. The camp keeps everything gated, right?"

Olivia watched the logic sink in. It became more solid in her own mind as she explained it to them. She wondered why they hadn't thought of it earlier. You didn't build a big old summer place like that just to be in the woods. A lake – or at least some body of water – had to be on the other side of the house.

"If there's a boat," she said, figuring things as she spoke, "we can lift Tock in and row across and that's that. There must be a landing on the other side somewhere."

"I see what you're saying," Preston said. "No matter what, we'll have water if the lake is there."

"But why would anyone leave a boat out here?" Tock asked. "You don't just leave a boat around."

"Actually," Preston said, "my grandfather leaves an old boat at Hudson Pond up where we live. He leaves it unchained, too. He figures anyone can use it and no one bothers it. A lot of people do that. The boat's no big shakes, so no one will steal it."

"It's worth looking, anyway," Olivia said. "We've got nothing to lose. Tock, you can stay here in case a vehicle comes along. Preston, are you up to do battle with the raccoon again?"

"I'm not going near the house," he said again.

"We'll go right around it. Maybe I'm wrong, but I have a pretty strong hunch about it."

"Still doubt there will be a boat," Tock said, "but if you want to go look, it's your business. Have at it."

"Let's wait a little for more light," Olivia said, "Then we'll go look."

Preston nodded. Tock shifted his leg on the backpack and let out a small, pitiful groan.

PART THREE
CALM

One of the most essential survival tips to comprehend, and one of the hardest to embrace, is the need to move calmly. Be deliberate in your actions. Because working toward survival is, necessarily, a high-anxiety situation, the natural inclination is to hurry, rush, try to get away from the immediate threat. Whenever that feeling builds, halt, if safe, and collect yourself. If you are with a second person, demand a moment to center you both. Rushing opens up a survivalist to mistakes, and mistakes can be deadly. Accept the peril. Accept the danger. Master it by calmness.

CHAPTER 10

At Camp Summertime, it took Devon O'Neal a twenty-count to realize the phone was ringing inside the main office. The ring started almost in his subconscious, then slowly, slowly worked its way up into his active brain. He had been in the boat shed, absorbed in fixing the motor on an ice auger, a tool he would need for ice fishing later in the season. It wasn't a job he really needed to do, not right then, but he liked keeping his hands busy, and he found when he worked on a piece of machinery he didn't have to remember how poorly his novel was going.

Besides, it was cooler in the boat shed next to the water.

But then the phone rang.

It jingled and jangled, and he realized, gradually, that he hadn't heard a phone or a bell or anything else for at least a day. That was the way he liked it, but at the sound of the phone he felt himself returning to the everyday world. He usually fielded a number of phone calls immediately after camp closed for the summer, some from kids who had left something behind, some from parents asking him to search around under a bed in cabin six or twelve for a retainer. It was only now, with the sound of the phone calling him, that he realized the phone had been silent since he had seen the owners off.

Strange, he thought as he threw down the screwdriver he had just managed to fit to a nut in the deepest recesses of the motor. Strange that no one had called, he reflected, until now.

He jogged across the camp common and stepped into the main office. The phone still rang. He picked up mid-ring and answered the way he had been instructed to answer.

"Thank you for calling Camp Summertime. Devon O'Neal speaking; how may I help you?"

"Devon? I can't believe I made it through to you. I've tried to call you a hundred times."

It was the camp owner, Mr. David Wilmont.

"Hello, Mr. Wilmont. This is the first the phone has rung."

"That's what I was afraid of," Dave Wilmont said, his voice agitated. "We've got a little problem. Did you know the electricity was out over most of Minnesota?"

"No, sir, I didn't. The generator kicked on, so I didn't know –" Devon began, but Mr. Wilmont cut him off.

"Yes, there's been a blackout of historical proportions over most of Minnesota. Historical proportions," he repeated solemnly. "Don't you have a radio?"

"Not really, Mr. Wilmont . . ."

"Well, you should have one. Crazy to be up at camp without some way to stay connected. It's been big news, I tell you."

"Yes, sir."

Devon felt his blood pumping up into his neck and face. He never liked confrontation, and he especially didn't like people telling him what to do. The entire point of being a winter caretaker at a camp way back in the woolywogs was so he *didn't* have to listen to people tell him what to do. Of course, he couldn't say that to Mr. Wilmont.

"Anyway," Mr. Wilmont said, "we've got a problem. People didn't know what connections had been missed.... Planes were grounded; trains weren't running. You can probably picture it. You can imagine what kind of chaos ensued during the blackout. It wasn't fun, I can tell you."

"Yes, sir."

"The reason I'm calling is that we're missing a vanload of kids. The kids Flash took out on One Hundred Mile Road. We're wondering if you've heard from them?"

"The Milk Truck? That van?"

"Yes, that van," Mr. Wilmont nearly yelled. "What other van would I be talking about?"

Devon felt his blood start to go into his ear tips. That was a warning sign. That had always been a warning sign. He had lost a good many jobs in the moments when blood went into his ear tips. When the blood reached a certain level, it didn't matter if the pope or the king of England wanted to yell at him, Devon refused to take it. Refused, and usually said something insulting to whatever authority wanted to tell him what he had done wrong.

He swung down into the office chair where Mrs. Wilmont usually sat.

"Now just hold on, Mr. Wilmont," Devon managed to say. "Just hold on."

"I'm sorry, Devon," Mr. Wilmont said, his voice rattled with irritation. "Sorry, it's been a frustrating time. The parents have been frantic. No one can locate anything because of the blackout, and the police have their hands full helping patients in the hospitals. . . . Well, you know how it can be."

"Yes, sir. I can see, sir."

Devon heard Mr. Wilmont take a long breath. Someone spoke behind him in a low voice. Mrs. Wilmont, probably. Mrs. Wilmont had a much better feel for the day-to-day running of the camp and the kids.

"Okay, so Mrs. Wilmont is here with me. Here's the problem. We don't know if the van ever got off One Hundred Mile Road, or if it's somewhere up north, waiting near the airport. We just don't know. Can you take a ride down One Hundred Mile Road and make sure they're not there?"

"I don't have a car, sir. I've tried that old gray van back in the horse barn, but it won't turn over. There's a note saying its dead."

Mr. Wilmont didn't say anything for a moment. Devon could imagine Mr. Wilmont's line of thinking. Deep down, Devon knew Mr. Wilmont didn't think much of him. He was just winter help, just an oddball who wanted to live like a recluse through most of the winter. In fact, the only leverage Devon possessed in their relationship was the simple fact that not many people wanted to live in a place like Camp Summertime through a Minnesota winter. Like him or not, Devon understood he would be hard to replace.

"I use a snowmobile, Mr. Wilmont," Devon explained, looking down at the grease spots on his forearm. "It's more useful up here through the winter. I'm sure you can see that. I get my friend Morris to drop me off and don't travel until the snow falls. I think you've met him."

Suddenly, Mrs. Wilmont took over the phone.

"Hi, Devon," she said, her voice braided with quiet and calmness. "Sorry about all this. You can see we're in a bit of a spot here. Seven kids haven't made their connections. At first, everyone assumed they weren't in touch because of the blackout, but now, you see . . ."

"Yes, ma'am," Devon said.

"Would it be possible to take one of the golf carts? I don't know how long they run, but you could take a couple of batteries."

"Down One Hundred Mile Road?" Devon asked, amused at the idea.

"I don't know if that's a good idea or not. Tell you what. We'll get back to you, but meantime, please keep an eye out. If you hear anything, let us know, please."

"I will, Mrs. Wilmont."

"Everything else okay?"

"Yes, ma'am," Devon said.

"Good. Talk to you soon, Devon."

Mrs. Wilmont hung up. Devon pushed back from the desk and got his breathing and blood under control. One Hundred Mile Road by golf cart. Sometimes it amazed him how stupid people could be.

Simon thought walking was not a particularly good use of his time. Not at all. He didn't like the weight of the pack, and he didn't like the mosquitoes that buzzed in his ears. He preferred to stay next to the fire. The fire was an excellent use of his time. He liked the way the fire smelled and how it was always in motion. Most people didn't think of fires as being in motion, but he did.

He liked watching the light build in the sky and slowly spread to the road. It reminded him of caramel syrup, a food he liked a great deal. Caramel syrup moved slowly and gently, not unlike the growing light. Now and then, he heard thunder, but it was far away and calm, almost like someone walking upstairs in a house while you were downstairs listening. Bess heard the thunder, he knew. So did Quincy, but they didn't talk about it.

"It's lighter," Bess said, her eyes up at the sky. "It's pretty cool the way it's getting lighter."

"This pack isn't getting any lighter," Quincy said.

"Just keep going. We can rest in a while. Let's make a good start on things."

"I'm hungry. I can't believe how hungry I am."

"We're all hungry," Bess said. "We all need some mashed potatoes, right, Simon?"

Simon didn't say anything. It felt too hot to talk. It felt like if you opened your mouth, the heat might go down your throat and live like a coal in your belly.

They walked for a while longer. Simon tried to understand why the remark about mashed potatoes struck them as funny. It didn't make sense. They had been talking about food, and he had named a food, and it was no more or less ridiculous than the foods they had mentioned. At least he didn't think so. Food was fuel, that was all, and what did it matter if you liked mashed potatoes or a club sandwich or caramel syrup?

After a while, Bess said they could stop. The light was strange now. Simon tasted the storm coming across the treetops. He tasted it on his tongue. And the wind changed. It turned the leaves upside down on the trees, so that you could see the underside of the leaves. They fluttered white and danced around. Some of the leaves, he saw, had already begun to turn colors for fall. He liked the fall. Autumn was an excellent use of time.

"How many miles do you think we've walked?" Quincy asked.

He lay in the middle of the road, his head propped up on his backpack. Simon knelt down. Bess told him he could sit, but he didn't want to sit. He wanted to kneel.

"Probably a couple miles," Bess said. "It's hard to say."

"Did you like that kid Tommy Elbow-Macaroni?" Quincy asked, completely changing the subject. "That was the rumor going around the boys' tents."

"No," Bess said, blushing. "And what if I did? Why would it be anyone's business?"

"I was just asking. Tommy Elbow-Macaroni told people that you liked him."

"His name is Tommy Elaconia," Bess said. "Not Elbow-Macaroni."

"That's what everyone called him."

"We were friends, that's all."

Simon glanced at his sister. He had heard the same rumor. He liked all kinds of people. Why did it matter if someone liked someone else out loud?

He was still thinking about liking people, and the various uses of time, when the first raindrops began to fall. They came quick and hard and exploded on the soft dirt of the road. *At least it might cool things down*, Simon thought.

"Now we're in for it," Quincy said, standing and gathering his things.

"We have a poncho," Bess said. "We can make a rain shelter in the woods."

Simon did not think that was a particularly good use of their time, but he didn't say anything. He picked up his pack. He also flipped up the hood on his jacket. A hood was an excellent use of his time, he reflected. A hood always followed you wherever you went, and when you needed it, it was right on your shoulders. Really, it was a pretty excellent article of clothing.

The rain came harder. It felt cold whenever it struck his skin. He pulled his hood tighter around his face. Sometimes looking out of a hood made it feel as though he were looking out of a tunnel.

"What's that?" Bess asked, lifting her hand to point.

"What's what?" Quincy asked.

"Those birds."

"What birds . . ." Quincy began to ask, but then it became clear.

Simon thought the rain had stirred up the birds and made them move. He knew immediately what kind of birds they were.

"Vultures," he said, and noted how both Bess and Quincy turned to look at him.

He nodded his head. He knew a vulture when he saw one.

Well, water is no longer a problem, Preston reflected. *Water is not a problem in the least.*

That was Preston's first thought as they came around the cabin. The lake spread out just beyond the house, exactly as Olivia had predicted it would. Light rain flecked the surface.

Preston also saw a canoe propped up on four cinder blocks. Someone had smashed a few holes through the hull, big bites that made the canoe look like a half-eaten ear of corn. The canoe's painter remained attached to a small cedar tree. Moss or lichen coated some of the boat's bottom. Its keel looked like a spine. From what Preston could see, it was an Old Town canoe, although the brand name on the side of the boat looked faded.

"What did I say?" Olivia yelled happily. "Didn't I say there would be water and a boat? There had to be! I knew it!"

"You called it," Preston said. "I admit it. But the canoe is history."

"This lake has to connect to our lake somehow. The camp lake. Don't you think? Doesn't that just make sense?"

"Probably so, but it depends on the direction."

"It has to," Olivia said, ignoring his reservation and hurrying down the last of the incline to the beach.

She stopped at the canoe. Preston came up behind her. The rain, he realized, had come and gone.

"It doesn't look like anyone has been here in a long time," she said, using her toe to touch the side of the canoe.

"At least we have water now."

"Skunky water, but I guess you're right."

"If we follow water, it's got to bring us someplace."

"Maybe we should stick to the road," she said. "We can't get lost if we stick to the road."

He nodded. "We need to go get Tock and vote on it," he said. "Do you think he can walk out?"

"I don't think so. He's hurt."

"You said you don't think it's broken, right?"

"Broken or not, he can't walk on it. Not very far, anyway."

Preston felt funny and nervous in his stomach. He wasn't sure why.

"Maybe we could all take a swim," she said, her eyes level on the water. "Maybe that's what we need right now."

CHAPTER 11

Bess couldn't look.

She felt as though she might throw up. The vultures stood around like a group of teenagers hanging out in a parking lot. They huddled around something down at their feet, necks tucked into their shoulders, the rain bringing out a dull tocking sound from their feathers. It was beyond gross.

"Let's get out of here," Quincy said.

"You want to go past them?" Bess said, her voice wiggling at the end of the phrase enough to let her know she wasn't quite in control. "Seriously, you want to walk past and see what they've been doing?"

"I don't like it any better than you do, Bess, but we've come this far. We're stuck out in the rain, and in case you've forgotten, something is waiting for us back in the van."

"Oh, this is so, so, so not cool."

She glanced at Simon. He hadn't said anything, but that didn't mean he didn't look. She knew from experience that he saw everything. He stood with his hands on his backpack straps, staring at the congregation of vultures. She imagined their garbled voices, their hopping up and down, and their squabbling intrigued him. He liked that sort of thing. She had no idea why he liked it, but he did.

"We're between a rock and a hard place, as they say," Quincy said. "But we have to keep going. We can't turn back now."

"We can if we want."

"You can just go by and not look, can't you? If that was Flash, he's not there anymore."

"It's just so gross."

Before either of them could say anything, Simon walked calmly forward. He didn't move his eyes away from the vultures, but he didn't stare at them, either. He simply walked straight ahead, bellying out a little when he needed to. The birds squawked and fluttered away, jumping like poker players disturbed from their game, and Simon waved his hand as he would at a mosquito. It was a warning to stay away from him, not a threat at all, and he kept walking once he was safely past the birds.

"We'll go together," Quincy said. "It's okay, really. Just look at the woods on that side, and I'll take the inside near the birds, all right? I'll hold your hand, even, if you want."

"Thanks," she said, but she didn't take his hand.

She tucked the jacket hood around her face and walked. She walked fast. She hated hearing the birds. And she *could* hear them, even though she did her best to ignore them. She kept walking. At one point Quincy drew in his breath sharply, and she told him not to look. She said he would remember it all his life if he looked. He said he didn't look. He said he was just walking.

One of the birds flew up close above their heads. Bess shivered and tilted her head down and nearly broke into a run. She hated the thought of them, their circling in the sky, their smug finality. She hated them all. She hurried forward and kept going even when she caught up with Simon.

"Let's just keep walking," she said to him.

"We're past it," Quincy said.

"Was it Flash?" she asked.

"Are you sure you want to know?"

She nodded.

"It was Flash," he said. "I'm pretty sure it was."

She went to the edge of the road and put her hands on her knees. She thought she might be sick. She smelled the damp pines and the dirt. Usually it was a good smell, but at the moment she simply felt overwhelmed. She had not signed on for this. None of them had. But all of them had been forced to march past a group of vultures.

"Are buzzards and vultures the same thing?" Quincy asked when she rejoined them.

"I don't want to talk about it. I never want to talk about it again, do you understand me? Both of you. Do you understand me?"

Quincy nodded. So did Simon. She pushed the hood off her head. It wasn't raining as hard now, and she needed to breathe.

"Let's go," she said. "We can get a couple more hours in before sunset. At least the rain brought water into the streams."

"The worst is behind us," Quincy said. "Think of it that way."

"I hope you're right. I'm so hungry right now I could chew off my hand."

"We're going to make it," Quincy said. "We've been through the worst."

Bess shrugged. He was probably right. She jerked the backpack higher on her shoulders and started walking again toward Camp Summertime.

Tock lowered himself into the water and tried to flex his leg.

It didn't work very well, and it throbbed like nothing he had ever felt before. He had always told himself he could refuse to feel pain if he needed to, but apparently that wasn't true. He couldn't avoid the pain of his leg. It burned and it ached and felt like it had been twisted like the top of a Tootsie Roll wrapper.

The water, at least, offered some relief. The rain had

stopped, more or less, and now the air felt a little cooler. He leaned forward and put his face into the lake. Preston and Olivia had already gone in wearing their clothes. They paddled around a little ways offshore. He sat back up and then splashed more water on his clothes and shoulders. It was strange to be the weak link. He never would have guessed he'd be the one to slow down the team. When the moose had charged, he had done the only logical thing while all the others ran stupidly in every direction. Being smart about the moose, however, didn't help with the missing step and killer raccoon. Now he had to depend on Preston and Olivia and he hated that.

"How are you doing?" Olivia asked him when she came back from her swim. "You feel okay?"

He hated *that* most of all. He hated being babied.

"I'm fine."

"Looks like more rain coming from that direction," Preston said, wading toward shore. "I don't like the look of those clouds. It's really getting gray off in that direction. We should get away from the water in case of lightning."

Usually Tock would have said something to mock Preston's worry, but he didn't feel up to it. In fact, he had to wait for Olivia to help him stand up. She gave him her arm and supported him while he balanced on one leg.

"That hurts," he said, hopping on his good leg. "That really wicked hurts."

"You can't walk, Tock," Olivia said. "We should just camp by the road and let you recover."

"If I keep moving, it will be okay," Tock said. "It's when I stop that it stiffens."

"You can't walk ten or twenty miles on that leg," Preston said. "Maybe we should go back toward the van."

"As long as we stay on the road, it doesn't matter which way we go," Tock said. "There's no food back there. We might as well keep going."

It started to rain. Really rain at last. Before they could come up with a plan, the rain sliced into them. It made everything more confusing. The rain came straight down. It was a hard rain, Tock felt, a dangerous rain. Clouds covered the entire sky. The sun wasn't going to pop through the cloud cover and save the day. Everything they had was soaked. For at least a minute, they stood dumbly on the shoreline, tucked back a little among the trees to be out of the rain. Finally, Olivia spoke.

"We need a fire," she said, touching the breast pocket in her jacket. "We need a fire just to get organized."

"I'll get some dry pinecones. That kind of stuff," Preston said, and went off along the shoreline.

"Tock, you okay?" Olivia asked.

"I'm cold."

"Help us get a fire going. We'll be okay if we can get a fire going."

"I can't walk very well."

"Well, do what you can. I'll build the fire right here. We have a little beach to work with.

"You think the matches are still dry?"

"We'll see, won't we?" Olivia said. Then she squatted close to the ground and began making a nest of sticks. It was not going to be easy, Tock knew. He hobbled around awhile, picking up dry twigs and bits of lichen-covered wood. He broke the ends off tree branches, the dead parts, because he knew they could catch no matter what.

"How do the matches look?" he asked when he carried the dry stuff back to where Olivia knelt.

"I can't really tell. I think they're okay."

"I wish this rain would stop," Preston said, coming up to join them. He had an entire dead limb of a pine. He withdrew a bunch of twigs and pinecones from his pockets and handed them to Olivia.

"Listen," she said, her face down to arrange the firewood, "if either of you guys feel you can do a better job with the fire, have at it. I'm no pro at this."

"You'll do fine," Preston said. "The main thing is whether the matches ignite. If they got wet, we're not going to have a fire."

Olivia cupped her hand and struck the first match. It flared for a second and went out at once. She set the match carefully on the pile. Tock saw Preston put his hand out to protect the small mound of dry wood that she wanted to light. Tock had a bad feeling in his stomach. He wasn't trying to be a pessimist, but the world was too wet right now for a fire.

The two matches Olivia tried next did not even smoke. They simply crumbled away.

"They're wet," she said.

"All of them?" Preston asked.

"We only have two left," she said, not looking up. "I wouldn't say all of them. That makes it sound like we have a lot."

"Should you strike them both together?" Tock asked. "You know, make one bigger flash?"

"That's an idea," Olivia said. "How about one of you trying it? I don't want to be the person who couldn't get any of the matches to catch."

Preston bent over to help, and when he did, water from his baseball cap spilled forward and hit the matches. Hit the ends of the matches, Tock observed. *Bingo, bango,* just like that. No one spoke. For what felt like a long time, Tock listened to the rain falling on the lake beside them.

"I cannot believe that just happened," Olivia said. "I can't."

"Sorry," Preston said. "I didn't . . ."

"Try them, anyway," Tock said.

Olivia did. They crumbled.

"That's that," Olivia said.

"What now?" Preston asked.

"Tock, you said you knew how to build some sort of shelter?"

"A debris shelter," Tock said. "We could do that."

"We have to get out of the rain," Olivia said. "I'm not going back in that house."

"Okay," Tock said. "Here's how we start."

CHAPTER 12

Quincy saw the road.

The other road. The road that was not One Hundred Mile Road.

The road that led to camp.

"Is that . . ." he started to ask.

It was still raining. He was wet and famished. He almost didn't want to put a name to what he thought he saw, because he suspected he wouldn't be able to stand it if he were wrong. Still, it looked like the road that went to camp. He squinted and tried to see more clearly.

"That's the intersection," Bess said, her voice becoming happy. "That's the road to camp."

"Are you sure?" Quincy asked.

"I'm sure," she said. "Can't be anything else, can it?"

"And what does it mean?" Quincy asked, finding himself walking faster. Walking as though to put a foot on the road to camp meant something important.

"It means we're not that far from getting to camp."

"How many miles?"

"Maybe ten."

"That's not too bad," Quincy said. "That's not bad at all."

"There's a chance of some traffic out here at least. Once we get through the gate, there's a chance someone could come along."

"Sweet."

"How are you doing, Simon?" Bess asked her brother.

Simon didn't say anything.

It took a few minutes to reach the intersection. When they did, Quincy ducked under the gate. The connecting road wasn't markedly different from the road they had been on, but it headed in a different direction at least. That was something, Quincy thought. That was really quite something.

For the first time in a long while, he felt like they might survive after all.

"Ten miles isn't that far to walk," he said when they were all on the other side of the gate. "We can do ten miles no matter what."

"I said I think it's ten miles," Bess said. "Don't hold me to it."

"Which means it could be shorter."

"Or longer."

"But it could be shorter," Quincy said.

"Yes, it could be shorter. The problem right now, though, is this rain. It won't let up."

"I'm not that cold. I'm hungry, but I'm not that cold. It's a nice break from the heat."

"Trouble is," she said, "you may not know how cold you are. It can sneak up on you. On all of us. Being drenched isn't a good thing."

"Do you want to make a fire?"

"Maybe that's a good idea. Maybe we should stop and make a fire. Just for a while. It could be hard to get it started, but there's always dry wood and twigs. Even if we spent the rest of the day here, we could probably walk out tomorrow."

"I'm down with it," Quincy said. "How about you, Simon? You like your fires, bro."

Simon didn't say anything. Quincy laughed and slipped out of his backpack.

And that was when they heard it. He heard it. It was a bright humming sound that you nearly couldn't detect unless you concentrated. He looked at Bess. She looked back at him. She held up her finger to say *wait a minute*, and then the sound grew stronger.

But the sound didn't fit. It didn't make sense. It wasn't a car sound, or a truck sound, but something higher and thinner. It sounded like a hair dryer, Quincy thought, or like a robot. Maybe an attack robot. He swiveled his head in the direction of Camp Summertime, and just as he did, a golf cart came skidding around the corner.

"Hey," Quincy said. "Hey, now."

"Yo, yo, yo," Bess shouted and began jumping up and down. She waved and then jumped on Simon and made him move around, even though he obviously hated it. But she didn't care, Quincy saw, and neither did he.

The golf cart came to a skidding stop a few feet away. The side of the cart said CAMP SUMMERTIME with the camp's logo of a sun setting on a lake while a few geese flew across the ball of light. Quincy didn't recognize the guy behind the wheel. The guy had earbuds in and a baseball cap pulled down far enough so that it bent the tops of his ears out. He looked about thirty, give or take, with a kind of dirty appearance. Quincy wasn't sure what to make of him.

"Holy pepperoni, are you kidding me? You the kids from Camp Summertime?" he asked, pulling an earbud out and letting it dangle. He turned off the cart or it stopped making noise. Quincy couldn't be sure. "You must be, right?"

"Yes, we're from Camp Summertime," Quincy said.

"On the Milk Truck?"

"What's that?" Bess asked, her voice dazed. She knew the name of the van, Quincy realized, but maybe she was in a little bit of shock.

"The old van?"

"Yeah, it broke down, and the driver . . . the driver didn't make it," Bess said. "And a moose attacked us."

"Do you have anything to eat?" Quincy asked.

"No, nothing on me. So let me get this straight, you guys left when the camp closed and you've been sitting out on One Hundred Mile Road all this time?"

"That's about it," Quincy said. "And there's another group, a group of three, they went the other direction. They're trying to walk out that way."

The guy whistled softly under his breath.

"Wow," he said. "This is off-the-charts screwed up."

"The driver died," Bess said, her voice wavering. "And so did the girl who got attacked by the moose."

Bess suddenly started to cry. It surprised Quincy. Not that he thought she couldn't cry, or never did, but she simply seemed too strong to cry. Not that crying was a sign of weakness, he quickly amended his thinking. Strong people could cry, and he couldn't really blame her. But she broke down, going onto her knees and putting her face in her hands. She had a lot stored up, he reflected. More than he knew. For at least half a minute, no one said anything. The three others stood and watched her. Then Simon, of all people, put his hand on her shoulder, and she slowly got control of herself again.

"Sorry," she said, wiping her eyes. "Just tired and hungry."

She looked up and smiled. It was a smile that barely broke through her tears. Quincy thought she might start crying again at any moment.

"I don't think I can take all of you at once," the guy said. "I'm Devon, by the way. I'm the winter caretaker for the camp. I can run one person up, then come back for the other two. It won't take long."

"How far is it to camp?"

"About seven miles. I'd try to take you all at once, but I don't want to overload this cart. It's built for two people and some golf bags."

"You can fit these two on," Quincy said. "I've seen three people in a cart before. One rides in the back. I'll stay here with the bags."

"You don't have to do that," Bess said.

"I don't mind. It's no big deal, honestly. You guys can get some food cooking. Get me some mashed potatoes, Simon."

That became the plan. Quincy helped them arrange themselves in the cart. It wasn't difficult. He piled all the bags together on the side of the road. Before they left, Bess hugged him.

"We were a pretty good team," she said.

"Listen," the guy, Devon, said as he climbed behind the wheel. "I'm going to have to make some phone calls before I come back for you. I'll make them as fast as I can, but just chill here and don't wander off. Stay right here, okay?"

"You got it," Quincy said.

Bess took the back of the cart. The caddie spot, Quincy had always called it. When he played golf with his mom, the caddie sometimes rode back there, standing up where the bag rested. It was a way to make short hops and to hustle the play along. Devon turned the cart in a small circle, then floored it. The cart bumped along the rough road, and Quincy watched it until it hummed out of sight.

Olivia admitted that Tock had a decent plan when it came to building a shelter. And like most good plans, it was all pretty simple. First, you found a tree with a *V.* That's what he kept saying: *A tree with a* V, rhyming it and repeating it over and over. Once they found a tree with a *V*, they searched for a long center pole and propped it from the ground to the notch of the *V*. That made a diagonal ridgepole, Olivia comprehended. Simple. If you thought of it as a backbone, all you had to do afterward was add ribs. The ribs formed the sidewalls. And when you finished with all of that, then you added debris. Leaves, branches, anything to block out the cold and moisture. That last part, adding debris, reminded Olivia of making mud pies when she was a little girl. You added and patted. Another rhyme.

When she stood back from the debris hut, she felt a swell of pride at what they had accomplished.

"Not bad," she said to Preston, who still knelt beside the hut, adding more debris.

"We need to get in and get dry," Preston said, not looking up. "We need to be out of the rain for a while."

"I'm not sure how dry it will be inside," Olivia said. "Better than out here, but not great."

Tock limped back from using the bushes. He announced his approval of the hut.

"That's a good hut," he said, going down on his backside and sliding in. It took him a long time because of his injury. "You could live through the winter in that hut."

"Is everything inside?" Olivia called to him.

"Looks like it," he said. "Come on in. It's okay. Try it out."

Olivia didn't quite trust the new, more cooperative Tock, but she had to admit he had improved. His injury seemed to make him more levelheaded, or considerate, though she couldn't say why. She went down on her hands and knees and crawled inside. It was drier inside, and a little warmer, although maybe, she thought, that was her imagination. Tock had moved the backpacks against the walls as an added windbreak. The pine boughs they had ripped off the trees and placed as a floor kept the cold and moisture from wicking up into the shelter. It wasn't too bad inside the hut, Olivia conceded. Given they had nothing else for a shelter, it wasn't horrible.

"Thanks, Tock," Olivia said. "Thanks for helping build this. You saved our bacon."

"No problem," Tock said, fussing a little with the sidewalls. "I used to make these things in my backyard with my buddy Blue Jean."

"He was called Blue Jean?"

"He always wore blue jeans is why. Blue jean shorts in the summer, blue jean long pants in the winter. He had a blue jean jacket, too. He always wore blue jeans."

Preston squeezed in before she could ask any more questions. He appeared tired and cold. He shivered now and then, Olivia saw. Despite the heat, if they couldn't get dry, it could become a problem.

"You okay?" she asked him.

"Maybe," Preston said, his voice chattering a little. "But that still doesn't mean we're not in bad shape here. We went from being on a road where we had a chance of being found, to being in a wet debris hut in the middle of the woods where no one can find us."

"You don't know no one can find us," Olivia said, trying to be calm and reasonable. "You can't say that for certain. And the house is right up there."

"Why would anyone be coming along this lake in a rainstorm? That doesn't make any sense."

It was a fair question, Olivia agreed. But it did no good to be more gloomy than necessary. Maybe they should have walked out to the main road before building the debris hut, but it had felt like the right thing to do at the moment. Meanwhile, the rain continued to splatter on the top of the debris hut and drip down on all of them. Olivia grabbed her backpack and propped it up so she could use it as a pillow. She pushed back against it and closed her eyes. She tried to send her thoughts to her home in International Falls. Her house wasn't grand by any measure, but it had a nice back porch, screened in, with an old-fashioned glider that was just long enough to accommodate her. Her mother kept an old quilt out there, and Olivia liked to lie on the glider, letting her movement rock her a little, the quilt tucked around her, a good novel on her belly for reading. Sometimes she thought the screened porch contained magic because she slept more soundly there than she did anyplace else on earth. Her naps on the porch, with the sound of rain, the coolness coming from the moisture, somehow pushed her deeper into sleep.

She felt that drowsiness entering her now. The one

thing she wanted, truly desired, turned out to be a piece of hard candy. Lemon flavored, maybe. She missed cracking candy with her teeth, the bright, solid explosion as the candy shattered and lined her jaws and gums. It was a funny thing to think about, she admitted. She smiled and felt sleep settling over her, and she sensed the boys settling down, too. No place to go. Nothing to do for the moment. *It almost feels luxurious*, she thought. Almost.

And she would have fallen asleep, except that Preston started crying.

It happened slowly, just on the edge of her hearing. At first, she thought he merely had the shivers again – which were bad enough, true – but then, bit by bit, she understood he was crying. He lay with his head facing away from her, and his shoulders sometimes moved and shook. She heard him trying to be quiet, but he couldn't contain himself. She felt horrible for him. She waited, expecting Tock to make some sort of mocking joke about Preston being a wimp, but to her surprise, he didn't say anything. She reached out a hand and patted Preston's shoulder. He moved his shoulder out from under her hand.

Then she fell asleep. She tried to stay awake, thinking that she might comfort Preston, but sleep clamped down on her, and her last thought was of the porch and the old quilt that sometimes tickled if you tucked it too close to your chin.

PART FOUR

MENTAL SURVIVAL

SURVIVAL TIP #4

Many survival manuals talk a great deal about equipment, shelter building, navigation, and so on, but they overlook the most important survival tool of all: survival mentality. People under duress can be tearful, depressed, uncomfortable, lonely, or despairing. The first job of all survivalists is to manage a clear mental approach to their circumstances. Stay positive. Look for hopeful signs. Believe that a better hour is on its way. Do not allow yourself to give in to low feelings.

CHAPTER 13

Bess twisted the shower water hotter and slowly turned in the steady stream. It felt like heaven. The heat, the warmth, the soapy cleanliness nearly made her giddy. In a few minutes, she knew, she could climb out and go to the supper that the caretaker guy, Devon, was cooking for them all. It was over. The entire ordeal was over even if it was a little hard to believe it had happened in the first place.

After one last minute of letting the heat soak into her bones, she turned off the water. Almost immediately, someone knocked on the door. She grabbed a towel and wrapped it around her and called to see who it was.

"It's Mom," Simon said.

Meaning, she knew, Mom on the phone.

"Okay," she said, and opened the door to the bathroom a crack so that she could take the phone. Simon stood and waited. He didn't like to talk on the phone, and seldom did, but he didn't mind listening to phone conversations. She shook her head no and closed the door.

"Hi, Mom," she said, drying and dressing herself as she kept the phone tucked next to her ear.

Fortunately, she didn't need to talk. Her mother talked for a full three minutes, asking and answering her own questions, angry one moment, joyous the next. It was classic Mom talk.

"Everything is fine, Mom," Bess said when she managed to dress. She wore a pair of jeans that had somehow managed not to get too wet and an Old Navy sweatshirt. "We did the best we could. It was crazy. There's still another group out there."

"That's what that man said. I've got a call in to the camp directors. The owners," her mother said, emphasizing the *owners* portion of the statement. Bess knew her mother wouldn't rest until she received some sort of compensation, financial or otherwise, to balance out the scales.

"It wasn't really anyone's fault, Mom. It was just a lot of unhappy coincidences."

Bess brushed her hair as she talked. She wished she had used cream rinse on it, but it felt good just to have it clean. The brush snagged and made her nearly drop the phone a couple of times.

"The van was ancient," her mother said, her voice tight with anger. "Ancient, Bess. I'm not letting them off the hook."

"Okay, whatever," Bess said. "Listen, Mom, I have to go eat. I'm starving. I'll call you later. Simon did great by the way. He really did."

"I'm glad to hear that."

"He did his best. He'll tell you about the moose someday."

"I heard a little about the moose. Did he get charged by the moose?"

"We all got charged, Mom."

After a few more back-and-forth pieces of conversation,

she hung up. Simon waited outside the bathroom door. She handed him the phone.

"Let's go eat. Then you need to shower afterward, okay? It will feel good."

He nodded.

Devon had cooked macaroni and peas, garlic bread, and he included hearts of iceberg lettuce. The meal looked and smelled great. Bess felt saliva start in her mouth. It gave her a weird feeling to be so hungry with food just a reach away. It was strange, too, to sit in the large cafeteria at one small table usually reserved for the camp owners or visiting family members. During the summer the place was a zoo, but now it was calm and pleasant. She saw Lake Monte out of the side window, quiet and calm in the late-afternoon sun.

"I am so destroying this food," Quincy said, dragging a chair out and sitting down. "I could do this meal three times and not be filled up."

"You maybe shouldn't eat too much too fast," Devon said, carrying the last bowl out from the kitchen. The bowl contained a quart or so of applesauce. Bess wasn't sure how that went with the other food, but she didn't particularly care. Let it be random as long as it was food. She took the bowl from Devon and put a big ladleful on her plate.

"Maybe we should have a moment of silence for Maggie," Bess said as Quincy grabbed his fork and stabbed some of the macaroni. "Just a moment, okay? Simon, can you put down your fork, please?"

Everyone went silent. Devon slid into the seat at the front of the table. Simon did as he was asked. It started to feel both sad and silly to be silent, Bess reflected. Both important and trivial. She let out her breath in a long sigh.

"Okay," she said. "Let's eat."

Then it was all just glorious food. She had never previously taken such pleasure in eating. At the same time, the food felt heavy and dulling. It chunked down her throat and seemed to ball up in her stomach. She wasn't sure why. It was as if her mouth wanted food, but her body resisted it. Quincy, she saw, ate avidly, but Simon wasn't shoveling it as rapidly as she had anticipated. She realized, watching them both, that they had been through something. It was easy to pretend it was all over, all tied up in a bow, but it wasn't. She felt a knot in her belly.

"So who's coming out, anyway?" Quincy asked while pausing to drink some iced tea–lemonade combo Devon had served. "Sounded like everyone but the National Guard."

"Search-and-rescue teams," Devon said. "And the police. Fish and Game. A bunch of people."

"Good," Quincy said. "You should be able to track them down."

"The owners are coming back, too," Devon said, pushing his plate beneath the lip of the mac-and-peas bowl and loading it with a second helping. "The Wilmonts. They're flying in first thing tomorrow morning."

"Are they in trouble?" Quincy asked.

"Not trouble, exactly. It's just that they're responsible. The blackout didn't help, but they should have provided better transportation, I guess."

"They should have better vans and buses," Bess said. "They think they can get away with old vans because we're kids."

"I won't say if I agree or disagree," Devon said, pulling his plate back. "I'm going to try to stay out of this as much as possible. It's probably going to get a little messy."

Suddenly, Bess felt herself nearly doze off. Sleep settled on her so quickly and so stealthily that it wouldn't have surprised her to have her head fall face-first into her plate. Her stomach felt stuffed, too, though she hadn't eaten very much. She slid back from the table a little.

"I need to lie down," she said. "I suddenly feel incredibly sleepy."

"It's the heat, probably," Devon said. "And the food. I put out sheets and blankets. You can grab any of the bunks just back there."

"Okay," Bess said.

She started to ask Simon if he would be all right, but even that felt like too much. She couldn't care any longer. She stood and apologized for not helping with the dishes, but she didn't really believe her apology, either. She shuffled across the floor and found the cot and fell on top of it. For a moment, and only a moment, she watched the light glance off the windows and a fly, high up against the glass, strike itself over and over against the pane, trying to get out.

"Are they wolves?" Preston asked.

"No, coyotes," Olivia said. "They're too small for wolves."

"Are you sure? Because we have wolves in Minnesota. A ton of them."

"They're coyotes," Tock agreed with Olivia. "We call them coydogs where I'm from. You can shoot them anytime you like. It's always open season on them. They eat cats."

Preston nodded, as if that tidbit of information helped in any way. The coyotes moved like spirit animals just out of sight. No, that wasn't true, he chided himself. If they were out of sight, then they could not be seen. These coyotes could be glimpsed, but only in instants when they trotted between trees or slunk through gaps of the underbrush. Then they flashed past, blending with the evening light. They could have been ghost dogs for all Preston knew.

"They won't attack," Olivia said, her eyes at the side of the debris hut in order to look out. "They don't know what to make of us, that's all."

She looked out and then turned back to look at them both. Preston tried to read her expression, but it was hard to do.

"A woman was killed by coyotes in Nova Scotia," Tock said from his own spy hole in the debris hut. "My uncle said the local coyotes are breeding with eastern wolves and making bigger animals. Canines. It's getting to be a problem."

"They're not going to come through the walls after us," Olivia said. "No way."

Preston didn't know what to think. He still felt embarrassed about crying in front of Tock and Olivia earlier, but he couldn't help it. Something inside felt tremulous and shaky. It was strange. If you had asked him who would be the most balanced, the most prepared to adapt to difficult conditions, he would have nominated himself. But things had gone differently. Things had felt different. Even now, squatting so that he could put his eye to his own little peephole in the debris wall, he felt nervous at the sight of the coyotes slinking through the understory. He felt if one swept close he might shriek like a little kid.

He listened as a coyote made one of its bizarre, painful yelps. It sounded like a strangled cat. It was horrible. As soon as one coyote finished, a second one took up the call and twisted it even tighter. He saw a big gray coyote trot close to the edge of the lake. It stopped to drink quickly then continued onward.

"I don't know if I can sleep with them all around us," Preston said, doing his best to keep his voice flat. "It's eerie hearing them make sounds."

"If they decide to attack, they'll come at us from all sides at once. That's how they hunt," Tock said. "Then they single out one animal and ambush it."

"So we stick together," Olivia said. "No matter what."

"We should each pick a tree," Tock said. "So that we can climb it if we have to. Look for low branches. A coyote can't climb at all. They're not like bears that way."

"I see my tree," Olivia said.

"Me, too," Tock said.

"Will you be able to climb with your leg? Or even make a run for it?" Olivia asked him.

"I'll have to, won't I?"

Preston didn't see a tree that worked on his side of the debris hut. He felt a tiny nudge of panic enter his bloodstream. What if there wasn't a third decent tree? That made no sense given how many trees surrounded them, but that's how it felt. He tried again to get himself calmed down. *What a raging wimp*, he told himself, but that did no good. He saw a coyote flash between two trees. He hated how its animal body looked: all belly-heavy and stick-legged. It looked like walking hunger.

"They're not moving off," Tock said. "That's a little concerning."

"I can't see a tree to climb," Preston said.

"Take anything, dude," Tock said. "Don't be choosy. Just find one you can get into fast in case these animals attack."

"They're not going to attack!" Olivia said sharply. "Quit getting everyone stirred up, Tock."

But just then, a coyote left the cover of the forest

understory and came toward the debris hut. It approached with only half its body; the other half remained poised to jump away at the least sign of threat. But it dipped its nose to the ground and made a breathy snuffling sound. Preston didn't think it was a good sign.

"They're getting bolder, see?" Tock said. "You think I'm kidding you, Olivia, but I'm not. They can be wicked nasty animals."

"They're not going to attack three healthy humans."

"I won't say they will, and I won't say they won't," Tock said. "But they're not here for afternoon tea, you know?"

Preston wished they would both shut up. He wished they were all home, all plopped down on a couch somewhere, maybe watching a Twins game, maybe eating a grape Popsicle. He ate a bunch of grape Popsicles during the summer. His mother kept them in the house, and she often said, "Why not have a Popsicle?" whenever anything got a bit strained in the house between her and her sometimes boyfriend, Harry. Things always felt better after a grape Popsicle, she said.

"Should we do anything to let them know we're not

defenseless?" Preston asked. "You know, make some sort of show of strength?"

He didn't like how the single coyote had come forward and seemed intent on gauging the danger in the lump of debris that had suddenly appeared in their territory.

"There's nothing we can do if they decide to attack," Tock said, lifting his eye away from his lookout hole. "Nothing except to take to the trees. I guess we could run to the house, but it's far enough that they would probably catch us before we got there."

"I'm going to go out and pet one of these stupid things just so you'll stop making them into a big deal," Olivia said, turning and sitting down more comfortably in the center of the debris hut. "It's ridiculous."

"They can come through these walls," Tock said. "Don't think they can't."

"Oh, now it's the big bad wolf and we're three little pigs."

"In a stick house," Tock said, his voice happy for a moment. "That's my point. That's exactly it."

Everything dripped. Preston heard a mosquito buzz near his right ear. He felt shaky again. He felt like crying. That was weird, weird, weird. He never cried, but now he felt an emotional wave sweep up along his body, straight from his toes. If he could have moved, he might have felt better, he reflected. Part of what drove him crazy was the sense of being trapped behind the porous walls.

"I need to get out of here," he said. "I'm feeling claustrophobic."

"It's in your head," Tock said.

He sounded like the old, jerk Tock, Preston realized. The nicer, gentler Tock had been an illusion.

"No, I really feel like I might explode," Preston said. "Like I might go crazy if I can't move around."

"It's in your head," Tock repeated.

"It doesn't help someone who is feeling something to tell them it's all in their head," Olivia said. "Everything is in everyone's head. That's the point."

A second coyote trotted up to the first coyote, the one closest to the debris hut. They sniffed each other quickly and then broke apart, each going in a different direction. Preston did not like the idea that they could be working as a team. He knew it was probable, but he did not like it. It made him feel sticky inside.

"Maybe we should head to the house," Preston said hopefully. "It's not raining that hard anymore."

"I'm not going into the house with the raccoon," Tock said.

"I agree," Olivia said. "We're okay here."

Preston felt words choking him. He suddenly scrambled forward on his hands and knees and went through the tiny igloo door for the hut. He kept going, crawling, until he was well clear of the doorway. Then he stood. His breath came fast in his chest, and his arms felt tingly and unattached to his body. He looked up at the overcast sky. He couldn't see anything but clouds. Darkness seemed to hold at the tips of the trees.

"Preston, are you okay?" Olivia called. "You shot out of here."

"I'm okay," Preston said, because he did feel better.

He hated it in the debris hut, he decided. It made him feel buried.

"Do you see the coyotes?" Tock asked.

"I see them," Preston said, turning to look in a circle around the hut. "I see them everywhere. They're everywhere."

"How many?" Tock asked.

But Preston couldn't answer. Two coyotes walked slowly out of the underbrush toward him. Both had their heads down and their teeth bared. Both looked as thin as pencils.

CHAPTER 14

Simon listened to the walls around him.

He often did that. Walls were more interesting than people knew. They contained more secrets than people suspected.

Right now, for instance, he heard Devon, the caretaker, talking on the phone. The phone had been ringing and ringing, and Devon had spent most of the night talking on it. Apparently plenty of people wanted to talk to Devon, Simon reflected. The phone also rang for other people. Plenty of people had been in and out of the cafeteria all night. Simon had never heard so many radio squawks. Everyone seemed to be connected to various transmissions that popped in, made sounds like a hoarse crow calling out danger, then fled. And everyone wore boots. Big, heavy boots that made a noise in the flooring that passed eventually into the walls.

Simon could hear plenty through the walls. He heard Quincy eating potato chips. First he heard the crinkle of a bag, then the grainy chuck of Quincy snapping his teeth through the chips. Quincy sounded like a horse, really, like a horse pulling up grass and mashing it before swallowing. The walls could tell you things like that.

Simon felt sleepy. But sleep could not beat noise. It never could. Noise always beat sleep. That was the rule.

His stomach rolled in a big, unhealthy wave. He put his palm flat on his belly's surface. His stomach made another grinding sound, this time one that went on for a surprisingly long time.

Simon pressed his palm down into his stomach. He didn't want the sound to enter the walls.

Then he heard Devon raise his voice.

"Well, don't blame me is all I'm saying! I didn't have anything to do with it! I'm just here . . . Okay, yes, okay, sorry, but I don't want this put at my doorstep, do you understand? This isn't my fault."

Then he said something about a newspaper calling for information. And a television station. After listening awhile, he hung up. It was late, Simon knew. It was very late.

Finally, sleep could win, because noise had disappeared. The camp became quiet, and Simon felt himself floating away. He always floated away at night. Everyone did, and they slept on their ceilings, only they didn't know that. He slept on his ceiling every night, dropping sometimes like a yo-yo if noise came to wake him, then rising again, curling next to the light fixture, asleep with the world paused below him.

Olivia heard Preston scream.

It was a horrible sound. Immediately, she went on her hands and knees through the door of the debris hut. What she saw terrified her.

The coyotes stood ten feet away from Preston. Both of them appeared ready to tear out Preston's guts.

"Easy," she said. "Don't make a move."

Tock came out beside her. They stood defenseless in the face of the coyotes. Tock could barely move.

"Make yourself bigger," Olivia said, remembering something her cousin had told her once. "Raise your hands up and lift your coat so that it looks crazy. Make it into a sail. They don't like anything that looks different."

She watched Preston do as she had recommended. The coyotes retreated a step or two and glanced sideways.

There are twenty coyotes here, Olivia realized, scanning the area in the near-darkness. *Twenty at least.*

"We should get into the trees," Tock said quietly. "They're going to come at us. Look at them. They're all over the place."

They were, Olivia saw. Except for the pair directly in front of Preston, it was difficult to gauge how many coyotes occupied the small wedge of land between the debris hut and the lake. Now and then, she caught a flash of their eyes. Their eyes frightened her.

"I'm afraid to move," Preston said, his voice shaky. "I feel like they'll charge if I move."

"They'll come from the side," Tock said. "You won't see the ones that come for you. The ones in front of you are simply holding you to a position while the others surround you."

"It doesn't help to know that," Preston said. "What should I do? I can't stand like this forever."

The coyotes were only steps away from Preston, Olivia observed. They would be on him in seconds if they decided to act. It all felt primitive. Humans versus animals. Omnivores versus carnivores. The coyotes didn't want to hurt Preston. They merely wanted to eat him.

"On the count of three, let's take to the trees," Olivia said, deliberately keeping her voice soft and calm. "Just walk, don't run. Running might spur them to attack."

"I don't have a tree," Preston said, his voice constricted. "I couldn't find one."

"You can use mine," Olivia said, trying to keep everything even. "It's the pine tree right to our left. Maybe ten or twenty strides away. We can go right up the tree together. We'll be okay if we can get to the trees."

"Start counting," Tock said. "They're coming closer."

"We're not a natural prey," Preston said. "They don't know what to do about us."

"They're hungry, though," Tock said. "You can feel how hungry they are."

"One," Olivia said.

"They're going to attack if I move," Preston said. "I know they will."

"You don't know that," Tock said. "I'm the one they'll go after, with my leg and all."

"Two," Olivia said.

The coyotes facing Preston crept forward. They had a sideways slink to them, as if they wanted to attack but couldn't quite persuade themselves to do it. It felt like standing in the center of a molecule; the coyotes were wild electrons and Preston was the stationary nucleolus.

"Walk slowly, *three*," Olivia said.

Preston walked toward her tree, Olivia saw. She walked behind him. It was hard not to run. She saw Tock limping his way to a different tree, one maybe twenty yards from the one she selected.

"Easy," she said, because the desire to run was intense.

"They're right next to me," Preston said.

"Just don't meet their eyes," Tock said.

Olivia turned her head enough to see Tock step into a beech tree. It was that simple. No coyote had threatened him or approached him. He climbed up two branches and then disappeared in the tree's dense cover. He climbed awfully well for a kid with a banged up leg. It must have been from years of practice.

It was night, she suddenly realized. A humid, rainy night.

Then, nearly at her feet, she heard a coyote snarl. And in the next second, the pack attacked.

CHAPTER 15

Tock watched. He couldn't see everything due to the poor lighting, but what he saw unnerved him.

Preston went down under a pile of coyotes.

Not one, not two, not three. A pile of them, all of them squirming and yelping and making sounds like mad people fighting over food. They sounded other-earthly, and Tock shouted to Preston to get up in the tree, but the coyotes covered him and wouldn't let him up.

Next, he heard a loud yelp, then a second one. The sound came from the center of the pack, and it took Tock an instant to realize Olivia had waded into the heart of the pack and swung a branch back and forth, clubbing the animals. She clubbed them hard, and each time she connected, the coyotes made a high-pitched yelp that sent a chill down his back. But whenever a coyote backed off, another one took its place.

"Tock, help!" Olivia screamed.

She kept swinging the club.

Tock wanted to help. He really did. He even turned to step down out of the tree, but as he did, he saw a coyote pass by and understood he did not want to end up like Preston, the center of a whirling mass of teeth and claws.

"I'm coming," Tock said, not so much lying as speaking to his intent. His good intent. He *wanted* to go help, he *knew* he should, but his body wouldn't follow his commands. He stayed half committed, one leg dangling toward the next branch. The coyotes made a horrible, horrible racket. He hesitated.

Then suddenly Tock saw Preston on his knees. He had managed to push himself off the ground. Olivia stood in front of him, still swinging her branch at anything that came close. She reached out a hand and helped Preston to his feet.

"Get in the tree. Now!" she commanded. "Now!"

Preston staggered to the pine tree and climbed up the first three branches. He could hardly hold on, Tock saw. Olivia backed her way to the tree, still swinging the branch. Tock swiveled himself around so that he could see better.

"You got it, Olivia," he said. "Just get up in the tree."

But a coyote slashed in and grabbed her leg. It bit and made a strangled sound. Olivia swung down at it with the branch but missed. She nearly fell but caught herself with the aid of the pine branches. Then another coyote hit her. Tock saw the coyote launch itself up Olivia's body toward her throat. She brushed it away as you would a spider you found on your shirt. The coyote fell and latched itself onto her ankle. But before it could do anything else, Olivia pulled herself into the tree. The coyote stayed on the ankle for a moment, then finally dropped free like a dull, gray piece of fruit.

"Are you guys okay?" Tock called. "Are you bleeding?"

They didn't answer. He heard their voices, but he couldn't make out what they said. He tried to see the coyotes, but they were even more ghostly now in the complete darkness. Occasionally, he spotted one, but they moved almost invisibly among the trees. *Like sharks*, he thought. The trees were boats and the forest was a sea and the coyotes were sharks, circling.

"Preston is bleeding," Olivia said eventually. "So am I. It's hard to tell how bad it all is. I can't see in this light."

"Just stay in the tree," Tock said.

A pause followed. Then Olivia said something. It was sarcastic: "I kind of figured it was a good idea to stay in the tree."

"Preston, can you hold on?" Tock asked, ignoring Olivia.

Preston didn't answer. Tock knew if Preston fell out of the tree into the whirl of coyotes, he wasn't likely to make it out again. Tock felt the branches already digging into his butt and feet. It was going to be a long night. A truly long night.

"Are they staying around the tree?" Olivia called. "Tock, can you see? Are they right around us?"

"They're all over the place."

"Tie yourself in, if you can. If you have a belt or something. You don't want to fall asleep and slip out of the tree."

"Okay," Tock said. "Good idea."

"I hate their sounds," Olivia said.

"Whose sounds?"

"The coyote sounds. The way they sound like children."

"Is Preston okay?" Tock asked, feeling he didn't have a clear idea about Preston's condition.

"It went for my throat," Preston said. "The big one. He went right for my throat."

"That's what they do," Olivia said. "That's how they hunt."

"If I fall . . ." Preston said, but he didn't complete his statement.

"You won't fall. No one's falling. We're going to stay up in these trees until we have a better idea of what's going on," Olivia said. "Trust me."

Tock felt as though he should say something. He needed to say why he hadn't immediately jumped in when Olivia called him. He had chickened out. He could switch it around in his mind any way he liked, but facts were facts: Given a chance to be heroic, he had clung to the tree and thought about how not to volunteer. Maybe that was smart, or maybe it was simple self-preservation, but he understood he would have to live with that knowledge – his chicken identity – from this point forward. It bothered him to think about it. He wondered if maybe everyone was part chicken, part lion.

"Sorry," he said.

No one answered from the other tree.

Quincy threw up in the middle of the night. It was the rich food he had eaten, he knew, but it was almost worth it. At least it wasn't like it could be if you had the flu and you had to upchuck a half dozen times, your guts straining like crazy. No, he simply walked in the bathroom, got sick, then washed his mouth out with a finger of toothpaste and headed back to bed.

He had almost made it back to bed, too, when Devon appeared with two other people who wore search-and-rescue gear. They were majorly rigged out, complete with two-way radios and yellow outdoor jackets that glistened in the dim light of the hallway. Devon stepped forward and spoke quietly to him.

"Could you come back out and tell us again where you think the other team went?" Devon asked.

"I already told you," Quincy said.

His stomach still wasn't great.

"I know you did," one of the search-and-rescue guys said. His voice was high and thin, and it surprised Quincy to see that the search-and-rescue guy wasn't that much older than he, Quincy, was. The guy was only a teenager. That struck him as odd.

"They just went the other way on One Hundred Mile Road. Or One Hundred Acre Road. Whatever."

"Can you give us more information about what they took?" the second search-and-rescue person said. It was a woman. She was tall and middle-aged, and her hair had tiny strands of gray in it. She seemed very calm, nearly to the point of boredom. But she also had a sense of competency, Quincy figured. If anyone found Olivia's group, it would probably be this woman.

"I'd like to help if I could, but I've already told you everything."

"You said they didn't have food," the young guy said.

"No one had food!" Quincy said, slightly annoyed that they wouldn't accept what he had told them. "I've told you all this. We had a little food and divided it up, then ate it pretty much."

The woman stepped forward and put her hand on Quincy's shoulder. Her hand felt cold.

"Here's the thing," she said. "We're having trouble locating them. We've been up and down the road, and we've come up with nothing. No results. So now we're back taking it around again. Thinking it through, you see what I mean? Sometimes a small detail can help us locate what we need. You never know what the small detail might be, but it's usually there."

Quincy tried to think of any significant detail he might have overlooked, but he came up blank. His stomach rolled deep down below his beltline. He felt weird and a little nervous, and the lights – they had a bunch of vehicles out in the camp, all of them with orange or blue flashers twirling around – stirred everything up. It felt like an alien invasion.

"Olivia said they were going to go straight out on the

road," Quincy said. "That was her last instruction to us. If anyone came to get us, that's what we were supposed to tell them. Right on the road."

"Okay, thanks," the woman said. "You hit the hay. Don't worry, we're going to find them."

"Hope so," Quincy said, and wandered back toward his bed. His stomach made a low grumbling sound, but he fell back asleep before he could worry much about it.

CHAPTER 16

Preston could no longer hold on. That was okay. He had tried and failed, and there was no dishonor in that. He was pretty sure he was bleeding badly, because sometimes he felt something shift in his body. It was almost as if his body contained a tidal wash of seawater and gravity. The moon, he thought, could change the blood inside him. He had never known that before. It was very interesting to know that, and he wished he could think more about it, but it was too late for that.

Sorry, I must be going, he thought.

That was a punch line to an old joke, but he couldn't remember what the start of the joke might be. *Sorry, I must be going.* It made him smile to recall it. And, really, if he had to fall out of the tree, if the coyotes had to get him, well, what could you say about that? The only expression that made any sense was, *Sorry, I must be going.*

"I don't think I can hold on," Preston said.

Or *maybe* he said it. He couldn't say for sure if he spoke or not. He wanted to speak, but his head felt cloudy. He had tied his one good arm to the pine branch with his belt, but he doubted the belt could hold him if he fell. He didn't want to think about dangling halfway out of the tree and coyotes leaping up to get him. No, it would be better to untie the belt, to be free to go if you had to go, because really, *I must be going.*

He smiled at that. Blood rocked around inside his body.

When he looked down, he saw the coyotes pass under the tree. They knew what awaited them. He had no doubt about that.

"How we doing?" Tock called from somewhere in the forest.

Preston didn't have a clear idea of where Tock was located.

"It's getting lighter," Olivia said. "How many can you spot?"

"I can see three," Tock said. "The big one is back under you. Patient little buggers, aren't they? They're in no rush."

"Just hold on," Olivia said.

Sorry, I must be going, Preston thought.

It was really not that hard. You simply let go. You simply surrendered. Then, once that happened, you didn't have to worry anymore. The coyotes took care of the rest. Right? Wasn't that right? He wished he could ask Olivia, but he wasn't certain his tongue still worked. Maybe it did. It was hard to say.

He reached up and checked his belt. His fingers undid it. He dropped the belt to the ground. A coyote came over quickly and smelled it. Then it retreated again into the understory.

Sorry, I must be going, Preston thought finally.

He let his hand drop from the branch where he had secured it with the belt. The sudden liberty of his arm threw his body off balance. He began to fall, slowly, remarkably, piece by piece. First his hand, then his leg slid off the branch. He caught himself with his other hand, but his balance was forfeit now. It was the seawater in his body pulling him downward. Something hard hit him on the wrist, then his foot slid off the last tree branch, and it was not far to fall. Not at all. It was just a little way, just into the sea beneath them, and he did not hate the coyotes, he did not even fear them.

And he was well on his way when the first rescue person appeared under the tree.

"Hey!" Olivia shouted. "Hey, up here."

Preston couldn't stop his fall. He landed with a soft *umph* against the tree branches. When his vision cleared, he saw a woman in a yellow jacket bend over him.

"You didn't stick to the road," she said. "Did you?"

"I guess not," he said, amazed at what had happened. *Sorry, I must be going.*

The rain comes. The water stays.
You can't leave.

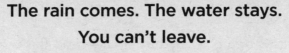

STAY ALIVE

F L O O D

Who will survive?

"Well now, look at that," G-Mom said, finally shuffling into the bakery. "It's flooding, isn't it?"

"That's what I was trying to tell you."

G-Mom nodded and kept shuffling straight across the room. She went to the front window and looked out. Kuru almost laughed to see her. G-Mom looked like an old turtle, or a chicken, turning her head this way and that, trying to get her eyes zoomed in on the water.

"Something must have broke," G-Mom said finally, pulling back as though nothing had been determined until she had witnessed the water herself.

"That's what I thought."

More water had come under the door even in the last few minutes, Kuru saw. She grabbed the broom from behind the cookie counter and tried to sweep the water out. But it did no good. If anything, more water followed the sweeps back inside.

"Give your mama a call and see what she says," G-Mom said. "I'll turn to the news."

"And miss your stories?" Kuru said, teasing her grandmother.

"That Illinois River is famous for flooding. You mark my word, that's what's happening."

"I'll call her . . ." Kuru said, then stopped when the electricity cut out.

It went out in one large *humppphhhh*. Then something made a loud cracking sound, the lights flashed for a second, and finally everything cut out again.